Matthew's Twin

First published in 2023 by Leilanie Stewart

Matthew's Twin Copyright © 2023 Leilanie Stewart

Cover design and internal artwork © 2023 Leilanie Stewart

ISBN: 9781739481902

Thank you for supporting independent publishing.

Website: www.leilaniestewart.com
F: facebook.com/leilaniestewartauthor
Twitter: @leilaniestewart
Instagram: @leilaniestewartauthor

MATTHEW'S TWIN

LEILANIE STEWART

ALSO BY LEILANIE STEWART

To my two fellow horror lovers, Joe and KJ

PROLOGUE

Night fell across Carraig Fhearghais Castle, but not darkness. The sky glowed with orange flames and thick, grey smoke spiralled upwards. Screams filled the air and the howls of dogs. The Scottish soldiers had ravaged everything within the town walls, starting with the church, which they had looted. The church, the mill, all the wooden houses; everything burned. Only Carraig Fhearghais Castle remained untouched. One soldier stopped for breath, admiring the castle. It was different than Strivelyn Castle, where he lived, as that was surrounded by cliffs. Carraig Fhearghais Castle had a gatehouse with twin round towers, defending it by land, and the castle keep was built on the Rock of Fergus that jutted out facing the Irish Sea, protecting it by sea on three sides.

The soldier was sweating under his heavy, padded linen hose and leather-lined metal helm. He pulled the headpiece, coif and padded arming cap off, gasping for air and tucked them under his right armpit. After fighting, there were only two things he wanted: food and a bed for the night with a woman.

Maybe he was in luck; a woman stood in a shadowy corner between smouldering cottages. Why didn't she run from the sight of him, like the other serfs, fleeing the walled town for the fields and woods beyond? Quite the opposite in fact; she lingered with a smile on her face, her green eyes beckoning him forward. The soldier strode towards her. Although his mind screamed a silent warning, his feet weren't under his control.

His padded gambeson of wool and horsehair, along with the leather jerkin that fell over his shoulders and dropped to his knees weighed as much as a sack full of groats; he couldn't wait to take it all off. Over the top of his gambeson and jerkin, he wore a yellow tunic emblazoned with a red lion. In his right hand he carried a falchion, and in his left arm, his large wooden flat-topped shield, reinforced with leather.

He was one of many Scottish foot-soldiers, Edward Bruce's men, a sea of yellow and red that had swamped Carraig Fhearghais. They had been among the 300 galleys ferrying 6000 men from Scotland to Latharna on 26th May, in the year of the Lord 1315, ready to conquer Ireland.

But not tonight. Rest after travails.

"You're going to lose this war," the woman crooned.

He pointed his falchion behind her. "We've already won. Look at your town. It's burning. You're lucky you aren't too."

She relieved him of his burden; the headpiece, coif and padded arming cap that he had tucked under his arm and carried them for him. "You've won one battle, but not the war. Not yet. If you want to win, there's only one thing you can do."

"Aye, kill traitors to our cause – like you," he said, with a sneer.

She started walking down a dirt road, turning to offer a taunting smile over her shoulder. "I have something you need if you want to win – if you're serious, that is. But if you're serious, I need something from you in return."

In spite of himself, the soldier was intrigued. What did she have that would guarantee the success of his garrison, indeed even the entire conquest in Ireland?

"We don't need any aid. We're the stronger army. You watch and you'll see this whole country fall under our control, as it should be," he said, as he followed her forward.

She pointed at his feet. "Then why do you follow?"

Among the dark shadows of the alley, fear crept into his heart. He was a brave soldier, one of a strong garrison, who had moments before sacked the town. Yet here he was, afraid of the unknown, scared of a small woman in the darkness.

They had arrived at a wooden shack. The doorway was rotten, the bottom jagged where the oak had tapered into triangular points. The soldier stooped, ducking under the low wooden frame and followed the woman into her dwelling. He propped his wooden shield against the wall by the door and rested the falchion beside it. Instinct told him she wasn't his enemy; but even if she were, he could kill her with one blow, if he had to.

Inside the shack were items that he expected in a peasant hovel, and items that were strange to the eye. A low-set bed made of wood with a reed mattress and a patched, wool blanket was familiar as the same style of furniture in houses back in Scotland. Directing his eyes further back into the dull interior, lit by embers from a hearth, he saw a stone altar. Suspended above it were animal bones: fish, sheep, chickens, strapped with linen threads to the ceiling. On the stone altar lay organs of animals unknown; a heart perhaps, and small, dark pieces of flesh that looked to be kidneys. The smell of fresh blood was rife in the air.

"The omens are in your favour, but you have to give me one thing in return." The woman cast a sly grin at the soldier. She reached behind the altar and retrieved two items, one in each hand; a black stone dagger in her right hand and a small brown clay urn in her left hand. The clay urn looked to have been freshly made; the clay was still damp, not yet fired.

"What is this one thing, of which you speak?"

The woman glided forward in one fluid move that seemed as though she had floated. Or had he imagined it? She closed the distance between them and sliced the palm of his right hand with the dagger. He was stunned; as a professional soldier, his reflexes did not normally allow such actions to occur, never mind to cause him injury. Yet there he was, as though frozen, while the blood poured from his strong hand.

"What spell did you put on me, witch? What have you done?"

The woman caught the blood, thick and burgundy, as it dripped into the clay urn. "This will give you the power to win this war."

"What power? You've injured my sword hand. What power can come to me now that you've weakened me?"

She ignored him, rubbing the blood into the wet clay with her thumbs until it had all been absorbed. The clay looked a dark reddish brown.

"Success is guaranteed. But it will take longer than you think." She set the wet urn next to a gap in the wall of her hovel, where one of the wooden panels had rotted away, letting it bathe in eerie blue moonlight.

"How long?" the soldier said, starting to raise his voice.

"You will take the castle within the year. But the journey for your own personal success will take much longer."

"What do you mean by that? Speak in plain words," he shouted.

"You will fall in your quest for glory. But it will not be the end of your journey. In fact, it will be only the very beginning."

CHAPTER ONE

"Sonya? Are you home?" Matthew called up the stairs.

"Yeah, I'm here." She sauntered out of the living room, holding a bowl of cereal. "Tony gave me a lift."

"Tony? Is he the Assistant Director on this new dig?"

She munched her cereal, spraying crumbs all over the carpet "Site supervisor."

"Cereal for dinner, I see," he laughed. "No pizza?"

"I spent the last of my pay on my hair." Sonya touched her bob. It was a bright shade of terracotta red. Her pencil-straight fringe looked shorter too. "What do you think? Like it?"

Matthew kicked himself that he hadn't noticed sooner. The hall light was dim, but it was still no excuse. Things hadn't been great between them lately, and not noticing her hair would surely add another black cross against him on her checklist. What he thought about it would also stand against him.

"It's…" he trailed off, "different."

"Different good?" Sonya squeezed her tall, willowy frame past him and smoothed her hair in the mirror by the front door.

He tipped his head this way, then that way. "Yeah, I like it, now that I'm getting used to it."

Sonya made cow eyes at him. "In other words, you hate it."

"No, sugar." He put his arms around her from behind. "I just thought the burgundy colour suited your skin tone. But this–"

She smirked. "You think the red makes me look anaemic, don't you? Say it."

An image of Queen Elizabeth I, with her pale complexion and bright ginger hair popped into his head. He brushed it aside. "Ach, no love. It's very bright, that's all. You can wear your hair whatever way you like, you always look beautiful."

She scoffed then brushed past him and went back into the living room. "How was work, then?" she said, in a singsong voice; with more than a touch of sarcasm.

He followed her inside and sat in the armchair opposite where she sat, cross-legged on the sofa, with her black cat Jessie on her lap.

"Same old, same old," he said. "Some sheep today, but mostly cows as usual. I'm more knackered than usual though."

"What do you expect? You're busier than normal since those Brexit checks got stricter a couple of years ago," she said with a shrug.

He suppressed his annoyance. "You know I've been a Portal Inspector for nearly a decade. It's not like it's a new thing now that there's a border down the Irish Sea. People don't realise that over at Larne, we've always been checking animals that come in from the mainland. Only difference is that we now have to check all of them coming through, instead of only a handful, like it was before Brexit."

She jerked her thumb at a copy of the *Belfast Telegraph* beside her on the sofa. "Well, smartarse, your checks are only going to get worse."

His eyes rested on the page she indicated from that day's edition. A picture of Nigel Dodds, MP for the DUP at Westminster, looking grim and serious mid-speech. sat atop an article. The headline in bold jumped out at him: *Report 'debunks' PM's claim that Windsor Framework removes Irish Sea border, says DUP peer.* He snatched up the newspaper and skimmed it.

"How are those red and green lanes over at Larne working out for you then? Are they giving you more paperwork, sugar?"

He chucked the newspaper at her playfully. "The only red lane I can see is your hair."

"Ooh, that was a low blow. I'll get you back for that." She waggled a finger at him, in a mock threatening manner. "You'd better watch out or I'll head down to Larne at the next protest with my 'Ulster says no to an Irish sea border' placard."

A cushion fight broke out between them, sending Jessie diving for cover behind the sofa.

"In all seriousness, I think the Federation of Small Businesses is right though. I think there's going to be big trouble come October this year with all these full customs checks for the majority of stuff coming in through the red lanes."

"Not that we can do much about it though, with no Stormont. Who gives a shit about Northern Ireland, really," she pouted.

Depressing, but true. "Oh well, on that note, after I've had my cereal – since that's all there is for dinner – I'll grab a shower."

She grabbed the remote and un-paused the show she had been watching before he got home. "There's a can of sausages and beans in the cupboard too, though maybe that's not the best idea since you're trying to lose weight."

His hands fell to his paunch, which hung over his belt. "I never said that. What makes you think I need to lose weight?"

She kept her eyes on the TV, though he saw a hint of a smirk on her face. "It's just noticeable, that's all. I mean, in the past month your beer belly has really ballooned."

Was this for real? He sighed and pushed himself up from the armchair. "Forget the cereal. I'm going up to get my shower."

Sonya sprang to her feet, causing Jessie to dive for cover on the sofa. "Oh babe, I didn't mean any offense." She blocked his path to the door with her willowy, athletic body. "I didn't want you to *not* eat anything at all."

"I've lost my appetite. You're not the first to say something, the lads at work are calling me 'fat Matt'." He skirted around her and out of the living room.

"Don't listen to them," she said, in the voice that she used when she was trying to be soothing, but which actually came across as cloying. "It's easy fixed. You're lucky that you've piled it all on your stomach. You aren't fat – large – elsewhere, so it should come off easily with six weeks of the gym and a strict diet."

"I've always been big-boned, since I was a kid," he called down the stairs as he trudged upwards.

"Aye, I know, but you've put on about two stone in the past month or so – at least. I'm just worried about you, that's all. I suppose the fellas at work must be worried too, if they're making light of it," she called up the stairs.

Worried, his arse. He shut the bathroom door to block out her voice. As if to taunt him, his stomach twinged. A sharp, stabbing pain sliced through his gut, above his belly button. He caught sight of his reflection wincing at him in the mirror and steadied himself on the bathroom sink. Come to think of it, she had a point about how only his stomach was large. Without his shirt and vest, his bare chest looked flat in comparison to his protruding gut. His average-sized arms enhanced his bulging stomach even more when they hung limp at his sides. Aside from his large, barrel-shaped gut, he had normal proportions for a five-foot ten man. His eyes travelled up the mirror from his stomach to his face. Under his salt and pepper beard, and the shaggy mop of black hair that hung around his temples, his face was oval shaped with a well-defined jawline; not fat in any way.

Sonya was right; he did look about two stone heavier than a month ago. What if he had cancer in his stomach, causing it to swell?

"Babe? Are you alright?" Her grating voice floated upstairs and filtered through the closed bathroom door.

He started the shower to muffle her voice. "Aye, I'm okay. Just getting ready for bed."

Not entirely true. If he were honest with himself, he wasn't entirely convinced about the possibility of stomach cancer either. The pains had been getting worse over the past few months; and so too had the strange dreams.

The strange dreams about Carrickfergus Castle, then called *Carraig Fhearghais Castle*, in the 14th century and last night, the Scottish soldier. Yes, the soldier in Edward Bruce's army, that had landed in Larne which in those days was known as *Latharna*, during the conquest of Ireland. The soldier. And the witch.

Yes, the witch.

Headaches and strange dreams, coinciding with the pains in his stomach intensifying.

"I'll heat up the sausages and beans for you," Sonya said, piercing his thoughts.

"Don't worry about me," he shouted, then added in an undertone to himself. "I'm just in the bathroom, going a wee bit crazy."

CHAPTER TWO

After his shower, Matthew made himself a cup of tea and poured a bowl of cornflakes for dinner. Not a substantial meal thanks to Sonya spending money on her hair, not food. He chided himself; keeping score wouldn't get them anywhere. She tended to keep score, so he wouldn't. Two wrongs didn't make a right.

Maybe what they needed was to talk – to reconnect. Good communication: he would start there.

Sonya was still sitting on the sofa cross-legged with Jessie on her lap, watching a different, but equally inane show.

"Sugar, I was thinking–"

"I know, that's why you're so overweight. You were thinking of sugar," said Sonya, turning to him with a wide, mock-innocent grin.

He rolled his eyes. "Forget it. I'm going to eat dinner upstairs then go to bed."

She sprang out of her chair, for the second time that evening, in a manner that was quickly becoming tiresome. "Aww, Matty, can't you take a joke? I was just kidding around."

"Well, I wasn't," he said. "I wanted to tell you something serious. But, since you're not in the mood–"

"Don't be like that." She glided across to him and sat on the arm-rest of his chair, stroking his hair in a theatrical gesture of kindness that he appreciated, nonetheless. "Tell me what it is, I'm listening."

He took a mouthful of cornflakes, gathering his thoughts. "It's sort of hard to explain. I had a really mad dream a few nights ago and it has stuck with me. I can't get it out of my head."

She tucked a ginger strand behind her ear. "What sort of dream?"

"It was about a Scottish soldier. He was wearing medieval armour – you know, chainmail, big sword, that sort of thing. He'd been part of a garrison that had just sacked Carrickfergus town, but not the castle. He'd been thinking about food and getting laid after the skirmish."

"Oh, of course, as you do." Sonya rolled her eyes and flapped a hand. "Dirty dreams and thoughts of grub. Typical, Matthew."

He gritted his teeth. "Not me, you dodo. The soldier in my dream. So anyway, there he was in the middle of Carrick, which was burning, and he sees a

13

woman lingering in an alleyway. He thinks she's a hooker, you get me, but he doesn't realise she's actually a witch."

She watched him, but didn't comment that time. Pleased, he continued.

"The witch lures him back to her house and tells him that the only way the Scottish soldiers can guarantee success is to let her do some necromancy, but she needs his blood. She uses his blood and binds it with this wheel-thrown clay pot that she had made earlier that day."

Sonya blinked. "And what happened after that?"

"That's all. I woke up after that. But it was so vivid, it's plastered in my mind like nothing I've ever seen before. I mean, like, even the place names were medieval in my head – you know, Carraig Fhearghais for Carrickfergus and Latharna for Larne. The Scottish soldier, he lived near Stirling Castle, but I dreamed of its old name – Strivelyn. Like, what do I know about history, I didn't even pick that subject for GCSE." He took another spoonful of cornflakes.

"Were you the soldier in the dream?"

"No. It was like I was a ghost, just sort of floating near the soldier, seeing what he was seeing. They didn't know I was there," he shrugged.

She gave a tight-lipped smile. "Maybe we've been watching too many historical dramas. My love of archaeology is rubbing off on you."

A swig of tea, which was still hot, burned his throat. He winced against an onslaught of tears. "This was more realistic than a film, more realistic than even watching those live re-enactments we've seen. It was like it really happened, long ago."

"Shame you didn't find out what happened with the clay pot," she scoffed. "At least we know the outcome of the battle – the Scots won. That part's history."

She would know; she was a field archaeologist. Matthew stared at her, realisation dawning on him. His bowl tipped in his hand, milk and cornflakes sloshing onto the floor.

"Holey crapamoley – you're working on a dig – in Carrickfergus, right now." He ran both hands through his hair, still wet from the shower.

Sonya raised her eyebrows, her forehead wrinkling under her blunt fringe. "Aye, and what?"

"Don't you see? There's a connection. My dream must be true. It influenced your work so that you got placed on that specific dig."

She closed her eyes, looking weary. "No, babe. You had the dream *because* I work in Carrick, not that I got the job because of your dream. I started work yesterday and you only had the dream last night."

He shook his head. "I had the dream two nights ago, the day before you started work."

She gave him a patronising smile. "You knew I was going to be working in Carrick for several weeks since I found out I got the job. The idea was planted in your head."

He waggled a finger at her. "Your dig isn't on the medieval stuff, though. You said yourself that the trench you opened is from the 1600s."

Sonya stared at him, pursed lipped. He'd got her; she had no retort.

"Well, even if you did have a strange dream, and supposing that dream took place in the 1300s, that still doesn't mean anything. It was still only a dream."

It was his turn to pause. She only wanted to argue; no matter what he said, she would always have a contrary argument. Dream or not, he felt disturbed. It had seemed, had been, all too real.

"Okay, well even if it was only a dream, it's not the first. I've been having dreams of life back in medieval Ireland for a while now – about as long as I've been having pains in my stomach, say like, a month and a half or so," he said.

"Dreams are just the brain's way of processing everything we do," said Sonya, with a dismissive shrug. "If you ask me, you're under a lot of stress, both in body and mind. Mind because of all the Brexit border bollocks and body because of. Well, you know."

She cast a glance at his stomach, pressed her lips together and cocked her head.

CHAPTER THREE

Ominous grey clouds hung low over the horizon as the lorries offloaded from the P&O European Causeway ferry. Matthew slurped his coffee as he watched the first cattle lorry pull up in front of the Livestock Inspection Facility. He pulled his high visibility jacket on and grabbed his clipboard and torch while the Veterinary Inspector facilitated the cows being offloaded from the lorry into the holding pen. He was sufficiently caffeinated and ready for another day of work doing checks on the animals coming over from Scotland.

As he crossed to the holding pen, thoughts of Sonya intruded, causing momentary distraction. The new archaeological excavation she was working on in Carrickfergus was on the way to Larne, so he was able to drop her off unlike her last dig in Armagh. This was no reason for her to pop into his head, right in the middle of work though. He glanced up at the blackening sky. Rain coming, or an omen of more.

It wasn't his girlfriend invading his thoughts; it was where she was currently working.

His thoughts drifted back to 14th century Carrickfergus. A Scottish soldier and a witch, bringing a prophecy that she said wouldn't be fulfilled in the soldier's lifetime.

Scotland. His concentration snapped back to the present. There was a holding pen full of Scottish cattle ready for him to inspect. He needed to get his brain in gear and do his job; it had been bad enough that he had taken so much time off because of his stomach pains over the past couple of months. If he took any more sick-leave, he'd be sacked.

Matthew approached the holding pen and shone his torch inside to look for the export tags. The reddish-brown Highland cows inside all had button tags on their ears and he could read the letters, 'GB' followed by the number 826, the code for livestock coming from either Scotland or Wales. He took note of this then shone the light on the second button tag showing each animal's individual number. Everything in order so far. Now all he had to do would be to check that the health certificate was valid and signed by an Official Veterinarian in Scotland and the cattle would soon be ready for authorised entry into Northern Ireland.

As he counted the cows, he trained the torchlight on the animals at the back, making sure he hadn't missed a single one. The beam of light fell in the rear corner of the pen, where a shadow moved between the last two cows. He brought his face up against the metal bars of the holding pen and craned closer, straining his eyes.

A woman crouched between the heifers. Her mousey-brown hair was tangled, and her eyes bulged with anger, giving her a wild-eyed, crazed appearance as she fixed her glare on him. She wore what looked like a simple, linen nightdress, though it was a tawdry brown colour from dirt and neglect.

"Stowaway! Stowaway in here."

He looked around and was relieved to see the Veterinary Inspector marching across the concrete towards him. As soon as he turned back to the holding pen, the woman had gone. He flicked his wrist, directing the torchlight this way and that in the holding pen, but couldn't see where she had gone. The gate was secure, unable to be opened by anyone other than a Veterinary or Portal Inspector, so there was no way she had escaped.

The Veterinary Inspector shone his own torch inside the holding pen, but still the woman hiding inside evaded the light. "I watched these livestock going in myself, Matthew – it must have been someone who got inside after. Who was it? How many?" he said.

"One. A woman," he answered, his eyes darting among the cows.

He had never encountered a stowaway in his ten years of working at the Livestock Inspection Facility in Larne. As the Veterinary Inspector spoke to the lorry driver and importer, his mind roved the possibilities.

Could it be an asylum seeker, a desperate person who had tried to find passage to safety? He watched all three go inside and search the holding pen. When they came out a moment later, it was with puzzled faces.

"There's no-one in there, Matthew. What did she look like?" said the Veterinary Inspector.

He scratched his ear with the edge of his torch. "Brown hair, scruffy appearance. She was squatting down so I can't say for sure, but she didn't look very big. A small woman, Caucasian, maybe in her late twenties or early thirties."

"A woman?" The Veterinary Inspector's forehead creased. "Are you sure you saw right? You didn't imagine it?"

"I know it's early in the morning, but I know what I saw." His voice sounded huffier in his own ears than he intended.

"Well, she doesn't seem to be here now." The Veterinary Inspector threw his arms wide.

What was with the sarcastic tone his boss used? He took a deep breath to clear his thoughts, before he said anything that would get him sacked on the spot. But one thought got stuck regardless, making the breath catch in his throat.

The woman was familiar. He had seen her before, though it had been at night-time. This was broad daylight, but he knew her, recognised her face. Yes, he was definite he was making no mistake about her face. She was the woman from his dreams.

The witch.

Pain seared through his stomach, like a white-hot sword stabbing downwards from sternum to bowels. A wave of dizziness beset him in sync with the gut pain. Coloured dots of light danced before his eyes. His head felt heavy, as though filled with lead. The weight began to buckle his knees; he was sinking, fast, towards the ground.

When he came round, he found himself sitting on the tarmac. The Veterinary Inspector helped him up, his head still swimming.

"Matthew, listen. Would you do me a favour? Go home. Rest, and when you're feeling better, go and get yourself seen – by a doctor – or a psychiatrist, someone to sort you out. Just don't come back here until you've had yourself looked at, would you?"

CHAPTER FOUR

The witch cupped the wet urn in the palm of her hand and pressed the wooden stylus into the clay. She made linear marks, curved designs and interconnecting triangular patterns in rows from left to right, top to bottom. Once she had covered the entire urn from lip to base, she sprinkled rock salt onto the vessel, rubbing it into the wet clay. Next, she spoke an incantation in a soft croon:

"Graceful Goddess of the Lunar Light,
Cleanse this urn in the dark night,
For the men in conquest who call to thee,

Make them victorious, have them serve me,
Help drive the foe from our ravaged lands
Place their care in your hands,
Restore power in the name of our common alliance,
Banish those English and their defiance."

She set the urn in the middle of her hearth until it was consumed by flames, baking the clay hard. Once she had extracted it, using iron tongs, she placed it on the dirt floor. There, it was flooded by moonlight shining through a gap in the rotted wooden shack. With the urn finished, the witch threaded a leather thong through a small square of linen fabric, dyed purple for power, using an iron hook. She pulled the ends of the thong, causing the linen to bunch into a pouch then set it next to the urn.

As though sensing that someone was watching her, the witch slowly turned. In the flickering light of her hearth, her intense green eyes searched behind, then locked straight ahead into the shadows of her shack.

***

Matthew awoke in a cold sweat. He was startled as he looked around the room, panting until his breathing steadied to a normal rhythm. He wasn't inside the witch's hut on a moonlit night back in Medieval Carrickfergus, he was in his home on the Oldpark Road in Belfast, in the semi-darkness cast by the lamppost outside.

That dream, though. He gulped. It was as though the witch had sensed his invisible, watching form standing in the shadows of her shack. For a moment she had turned and locked eyes with him as he intruded on her private ceremony, making the clay urn.

Either he was going crazy, or there was a supernatural influence in his life.

The dreams were so vivid they *had* to be real. When he witnessed the scenes, it seemed as though he were a paranormal presence himself, a free-floating spectre seeing everything around, but as alert and lucid as in his own real life.

What about yesterday at work? Had the crouching woman, the witch he had seen in the holding pen been a dream too? Or was it a real visitation, a ghost, warning him of—

Of what?

What had a witch, and a Scottish soldier, got to do with his life in twenty-first century Northern Ireland? Matthew had no clue. He thought of the dream he had been having only moments before. Why did the witch care so much about the Scottish invaders winning the conquest? Wasn't it Edward Bruce and his army who were the invaders? What about the witch herself; she was a local, one of the townsfolk in Carrickfergus, not one of the Scots. In the previous dream he'd had, the one with the Scottish soldier who had helped in sacking the town, the witch had taken his blood and used it for purposes of necromancy when she had rubbed it into the clay urn.

"Matthew, what's up?" Sonya sat up in the semi-darkness of their bedroom.

"I think there's something wrong with me," he said.

She guffawed. "Yeah, I've been telling you that for years."

He didn't laugh. "No, I'm serious. I didn't tell you what happened earlier. I got sent home from work today because I collapsed."

"Oh babe, was it because of those pains you've been having?" He felt the warmth of her hand as she rested it on his stomach and started rubbing.

"No, not that." He paused, gathering his thoughts. "I just had another dream about the Scottish soldier and the witch. But that's not all. Earlier today when I doing my usual checks in the Livestock Inspection Facility, I saw a woman hiding in the holding pen behind the Scottish cattle. It was the witch from my dreams."

She groaned. "You know what I think? You're distracted because of your stomach trouble. I think you should go and get a health check. The doctor might even be able to recommend a dietician for you to work with, help you to lose some–"

"This isn't about my weight, Sonya." His voice was sharper than he intended. "My boss suggested a health check today too – but not a doctor. He told me to get my head examined. He thinks I'm mental."

She sighed in the darkness. "Over a couple of dreams?"

"I never told him about the dreams."

He felt her hand, rubbing his back. "See, you're getting yourself so worked up that you're even imagining you're seeing that woman from your dreams in real life."

"I didn't imagine it, though. At least I don't think I did. I swear she was really there, hiding behind the cows." He wiped his brow. His whole body was slick with cold sweat. With crisscrossed hands, he grabbed the hem of his t-shirt and pulled it up over his head.

Both hands jumped to his gut as a spear of pain jabbed through his core and he massaged his stomach. But what was that? His fingers found bumps across his midriff, about an inch above the bellybutton. The skin was raised like blisters, though he didn't feel any itch, or burning.

Matthew reached for his phone on the bedside table. He switched the torch light on and shone it on his bare stomach. Angry, red blisters, each about an inch in length, stretched across his middle in a straight line. The blisters were linear in form and as his eyes adjusted to what he was seeing, he read three words in Latin.

Veniam ad vos.

I am coming for you.

Sickness rose in his gut and he retched.

"What is it babe, what's wrong?"

"Look here." With his other hand, he pointed at the raised marks. But even as he indicated the writing, it began to disappear. Not even a trace of the red, raised letters that had been carved into his skin moments before.

"I don't see anything. What am I meant to be looking at?" She bent low, looking at his stomach where he indicated.

"Didn't you see the writing? It was Latin. It said, 'I am coming for you'. She's after me, that witch. Either her, or the soldier – or them both."

She laughed again. "Would you listen to yourself? Look, I'll go and make you a nice cup of tea. You're really shaken up by this bad dream."

"It wasn't a dream," he snapped. "I'm telling you, something really weird is happening to me and I'm scared."

He saw her wide eyes full of fear – and pity – as she switched on the bedside lamp, flooding the room with light. "Alright, I'm listening. But you know what I think? Your boss is right. You really should talk this through with someone who can give you more help. A therapist."

He huffed. "I don't believe it. You think I'm crazy too."

"I don't, I really don't." Her answer was too quick, too defensive. "I believe that you think you saw writing on your stomach and that you think you saw a woman in the cow pen at work. I really do. But maybe a therapist can make more sense of all of this. Don't you think so, babe? It's not weakness to get help when you need it, it's strength."

CHAPTER FIVE

"Sonya doesn't even believe me. I really feel like I have nobody to turn to who'll listen." Matthew sighed.

Gary watched him over the top of his Magners. "I'm sure it's just because she's worried. Not to talk shop too much, but things can get pretty serious, fast, especially if it's a bowel issue. If you were referred to me, I'd start you on wholemeal bread and pasta right away. You should think about switching from those cornflakes to bran as well, starting tomorrow."

It was useful having a dietician for a best mate. Gary always had good advice that he offered without sounding condescending. Granted, maybe that was more to do with being a nice lad rather than his work as a medical sort.

"You don't think it could be Crohn's disease, or bowel cancer?"

"You'd be bleeding if it was as serious as that – although I'm no doctor. You really should think about going for a check-up."

He took a sip of his Guinness and pondered what Gary had said.

"That's a good choice too." Gary gestured to his Guinness. "It'll coat your stomach, if IBS is your issue. It's rich in iron, best choice for any gut problems."

He stared at the froth on top of his pint, as though it would offer an enigmatic solution, hidden in the coffee-coloured swirls. "I'm only thirty-three, too young for a debilitating condition. It's clearly chronic – I've had a barrel-shaped gut and ribcage since I was a child. Seems to be degenerative too. I've got much worse in the last couple of months."

Gary threw up his hands. "What else can I say? I'm frankly shocked you haven't already been for a colonoscopy already. Better get on to your GP soon, the NHS is falling apart with all the cutbacks."

He scratched his neck. "Sorry for all the grim chat anyway, mate. I'll tell you something much more interesting this time instead. This would interest your Katie for sure – she's all into dream analysis, isn't she?"

"Aye, she's doing some research on the impact of lucid dreaming on memory and cognition at the moment, actually," said Gary.

"Well, she'd have a field day with this then. It's these recurring dreams I've been having lately, as in the past month. They're sort of occult dreams, like, there's a witch and a Scottish soldier, back in the 14th century.

He's in Edward Bruce's army and they've just landed in Carrickfergus, you know, sacked the whole town, everything burning. And then—"

His eyes fell behind Gary. Across the wide, crowded bar of men and women out for drinks after the nine to five, or students celebrating the end of exams, there she was. The only face not animated, not enjoying drinks or socialising. She sat alone, her mousey-brown hair a bird's nest, her wicked green eyes in shadow; and fixed on him. She sat in a straight line opposite him, her face angled towards his, as if no-one else in the bar existed except him. He choked on his Guinness.

"Matt, you alright there, mate?"

He craned his head a fraction to the left and saw a dark silhouette in a far corner of the bar through his peripheral vision. He strained his eyes to search the shadows; damn the mood lighting in the bar. The witch wasn't alone. There was no mistaking the man; it was the Scottish soldier – or the ghost of him – wearing a beige padded gambeson without the yellow and red tunic, in Edward Bruce's colours, draped over the top.

What did they want with him?

"Matt?" Gary's fingers snapped in front of his face, drawing him back to the moment. "Woah, I lost you there for a moment. You okay?"

He stared at Gary, though he wasn't really seeing his friend; his retinas had been burned with an image of the witch at one far end and the soldier in another shadowy corner.

"Aye, I'm alright, I'm with it."

"You were telling me about your dream and then you just zoned out," said Gary.

"I don't think she wants me saying anything more. I think I've said enough." He glugged half his pint in one go; the witch and the soldier had sobered up what little buzz he'd had going.

"Who doesn't want you saying anything? Sonya?"

Mention of his girlfriend snapped him back to reality. "Sonya already knows. She wouldn't care if I told anyone or not – to be honest, I think she thinks I'm nuts. No, I was talking about the witch. You know, I'm actually starting to think there's more to these dreams than what I'd been thinking."

"You mean – like the dreams are real?" Gary set his Magners down.

Matthew chortled. "That would be mad though, wouldn't it?"

"Not really. Dreams are a manifestation of what we go through in our waking lives. When we sleep, our brain has to process everything. So, if you're dreaming about a witch, then that's your brain making sense of a conflict that you're having with someone in your actual life."

"Sadly, that's true. Sonya and I haven't been getting on well recently," he sighed.

Gary pursed his lips. "I'm sure whatever it is will work itself out."

He shrugged. "I don't know. We've been together for twelve years, since we both graduated. I mean, hell, we even met out celebrating the end of exams over at the Parlour for drinks – her archaeology lot from Queen's and my business crew from Ulster. We've lived together for ten of those twelve years, but that's just it. There's no real spark anymore between us. No talk of tying the knot, or kids, nothing. No commitment. I can't tell if she's stringing me along, waiting for something better, or is comfortable as we are."

"Have you told her all of this?"

"I've tried a few times, but she just laughs it off and changes the topic," he said. "It's always like, 'awk babe, you're always so serious and boring' or 'here we go again, the same old silly worries'. I swear she just trivialises everything and gets defensive. At this point, I don't even know what she's thinking, what makes her tick."

Gary blinked at him and said nothing. That about summed it up; what was there to say?

He felt bad. Was it a betrayal to talk behind Sonya's back like that, to deride his life partner of the past dozen years? He'd known Gary almost as long; they'd been housemates together when he'd started his first permanent job eleven years before, but he'd never told Gary the bare bones of things with Sonya. Gary had only met Sonya in person on one occasion, in fact: when they'd attended his wedding to Katie. Relationships were private, should only have been discussed between the people involved. Of course, the way things were going, he wouldn't be in a relationship with Sonya much longer in any event.

"It sounds like she's mostly worried about your health and that must be putting a dampener on things. Maybe if you get yourself an appointment booked and then talk things through with her to reassure her you're getting help, she'll come round."

CHAPTER SIX

The wind funnelling down from the top of Cavehill had to be gale force. Matthew could barely keep his eyes open as they climbed the path behind Belfast Castle. Tears streamed across his temples and his hair was whipped back from his face.

"Brisk, isn't it?" Sonya smirked.

Usual sarcasm then; at least she was in good form. When her comments were cold and clipped, that was when he had to worry. Nothing between them could be that bad if she was still making light of things.

"Aye, it's fresh alright," he agreed.

"We're lucky we live so close to this place. How many people can live in a city and still be within walking distance of a country park?

Cavehill country park wasn't too long a walk from their house on the Oldpark Road. If he had got his way, they would have been parking the car in front of the castle and taking a short dander up, but then it only would've given Sonya more ammunition to make comments about how overweight and unfit he was to want to drive for a few minutes. He had buttoned his lip and put on his work boots for the hike – and let her lead the way.

They climbed up higher through the trees behind Belfast Castle and across a landslide, where the dried mud was powdery, towards Napoleon's Nose. It made him huff and puff. Was she taking him on a deliberately difficult route as a way of punishing him because she believed he was overweight and unfit and needed exercise? As she clambered ahead of him, he could see that she was in amazing shape. Her willowy body was an array of lean, muscular limbs as she climbed: long legs and archaeology-honed arms found grooves within the rocky landslide to place her hiking boots and nodules to grip with her spidery fingers, calloused from working outdoors on excavations for so long. She peered back at him, her face half in shadow.

"Keep up, slow poke," she laughed.

"Wanna give me a piggyback?" He sat to catch a breath, digging his heels into the powdery mud; one wrong move and he'd be slipping on his arse the whole way down the landslide.

She pointed at him. "You're filthy."

He looked down his body. An area the size of a hubcap on his stomach was coated with a dusting of fine, powdery soil. While he had clambered on all fours across the landslide, he hadn't been aware of his protruding gut scraping over the soil. As though aware it was on his mind, his gut clenched and a sharp, stabbing pain shot downwards. The nerve running through his groin felt aflame as the pain raced down his right leg and into his foot.

"Ow!" He rolled sideways and grabbed his stomach with both hands.

"Matty, what is it?"

"Another twinge. It's always in my right side."

She grabbed him under his armpits. "Let's press on to the top and then we can call 999 if we have to."

"I can't move though," he groaned.

"Work through the pain. Exercise might help get the blood flow stimulated." Sonya groaned too with the strain of supporting him up the slope.

"Not if it's appendicitis. If a blood vessel is ruptured and the infection gets into my bloodstream, then–"

"Now isn't the time to be thinking like that." For a moment he thought she actually cared; all that was dashed when she continued. "Especially when you haven't even contacted a doctor."

"As a matter of fact, I have. I called the doctor after I went for drinks with Gary yesterday. I have an appointment booked for next Tuesday."

She fell quiet. When they reached the flat basalt of Napoleon's Nose, he lay spreadeagle, panting. Sonya loomed over him as she caught her breath, her arms around her knees in a protective gesture.

"Is the pain gone now?" Her eyes travelled from his face down to his stomach, that even as he lay flat, remained as a solid dome.

Once more, as though it were a sentient being and not part of his body, his stomach seemed to be listening. In less than a second, the stabbing, jarring pain was gone.

He unzipped his jacket and pulled his jumper up over the dome of his stomach, bunching it under his ribcage. He clapped his right hand over his lower right abdomen, where the appendix would be. Hot, raised bumps, dotted his skin. His forefinger and index finger explored the welts; he pushed himself up onto his elbows to look down his body.

Veniam ad vos.

I am coming for you.

The message, in Roman letters, was the same one that had appeared on his stomach in bed, several nights before.

"Look, Sonya, see there? See those letters?"

Sonya peered over his body. She shook her head. "Letters? What are you on about?"

The red welts faded, but the heat in his skin remained. A moment later, right before his eyes, he saw new Roman letters appear.

Fatum advenit.

Fate has arrived.

The heat caused an intense itch in his skin. He scratched the blisters, rolling his head back with the soothing pain created by his own fingernails as they relieved the burning.

"You must see the Roman letters, don't you?" he said.

She shook her head again, slower this time. "It's very red where you're scratching, like you're having an allergic reaction to a bug bite, or something."

"Look closer. See right under my finger? There's a series of welts." He moved his forefinger a fraction to the side, so that she could see where he indicated.

"All I can see under the general red area you've caused by scratching is darker red lines."

"Yes, that's it. It's writing. Look closer and you'll make out the message, 'fatum advenit'. It says, 'fate has arrived'."

"I know how to read Latin, dumdum." She rolled her eyes. "I'm not seeing any Roman words, or any writing at all, for that matter. Those darker red raised bits are just stretchmarks, babe. You've put on so much weight in the past couple of months that your skin has stretched."

He let out an exasperated growl. "Why am I not getting through to you? This isn't all in my head. Something bad – paranormal – is happening to me. I could really do with having you on my side as I figure this out. There are enough people against me with my colleagues calling me 'fat Matt' and acting like my stomach problems and seeing the witch at work the other day, are all in my head. Could you do me a favour and listen to what I'm saying for once, please?"

She puckered her mouth, her eyes lowered. "Aye okay, don't get your knickers in a twist, I'm listening," she said in a fluster. "As a matter of fact, I do believe you. After you told me about your dreams of the witch, I decided to text Katie and see what she made of it."

"Katie?" He cocked his head.

"Aye, you know, Gary's wife. You were out with him yesterday for drinks? You couldn't have forgotten his missus already, could you?"

His jaw dropped. "I didn't know you were in touch with Katie. Since when?"

She sniffed, and he knew she was trying to cover her tracks. "We're not really in touch. I knew she did dream research, so I messaged her."

"How did you get her number?"

Her freckles darkened as a blush spread across her cheeks. "Do you want to hear what she said, or what?"

"Yeah, yeah, wind your neck in, I was just asking." He flapped a hand in a dismissive gesture.

She sighed, though it seemed more in relief than exasperation. What was she hiding? "If you dream of a witch, it's to do with having a conflict in real life with someone close to you. This dream symbolises a threat to you that you are dealing with. You need to set boundaries with the instigator of the tension in your life, so that the person involved will show respect for you. So, who is it, Matthew? Who are you having conflict with?"

He stared at her, searching first her right eye, then left, then back to right. "How did you get Katie's number?"

The blush in her cheeks, which hadn't quite faded, returned with a deep glow. "I got it from your phone."

"What were you doing on my phone?" he fumed.

Her bottom lip stretched downwards, and she averted her eyes, clearly thinking of an excuse to use to lie to him.

"Well?" he goaded.

Her eyes darted upwards; her gaze defiant at she glared at him. "If you really must know, I was concerned for you, so I went through your contacts to try and find the surgery number. I was going to make you an appointment – I didn't know you'd already made one yourself."

He pressed his lips together and refrained from saying what he was thinking: *Aye right.*

"So maybe you should know that I actually *do* care about you, believe it or not, before you accuse me of snooping through your private information." She stood up, dusted soil off her trousers and marched towards the path back down.

He opened his mouth, about to point out that if her intentions were good then why did she also take Katie's number out of his contacts? He vetoed that thought before it left his brain. What was the point? Sonya was mad at him, and would stay mad, until she decided not to be. Matthew looked out across the expanse of Greater Belfast spread below imagining medieval soldiers running amok, burning and looting, and above it all, the unseen hand of witchcraft steering their fate.

CHAPTER SEVEN

Matthew lay on the gurney in his doctor's office. He clasped his hands over the large dome of his stomach, feeling self-conscious. She hadn't yet given him the lecture about how he needed to lose weight and do exercise, but he was expecting it. Everyone lately did it: his colleagues, his friends, his family. Sonya was the worst. At least this would make her happy. She couldn't berate him any longer for not seeing the doctor and hopefully it would be the first step towards them repairing the communication gap in their relationship.

The doctor came back into the room with a new blood pressure monitor and strapped it to his arm. "How long did you say you've been having these stomach problems?"

He stared at the ceiling lights as he thought. "Do you mean historically, or lately?"

The doctor's mouth puckered. "Do you have a family history of any serious stomach illnesses – ulcerative colitis, bowel cancer, or Crohn's disease?"

"None that I know of, though you read my mind – I'd been starting to think I had one of those scary diseases myself. Google throws up the worst illnesses when you try to look anything up, it would scare the crap out of you." He laughed.

Didn't seem like his feeble attempts at lightening the mood were working; the doctor remained stoic as she pumped the blood pressure monitor and let it deflate. "What have been your symptoms recently?"

He sniffed. "Well, my abdomen and ribcage has swollen to these abnormal proportions, and I've been getting a lot of pain, especially in the lower right area."

"Any bleeding when you pass stools?"

He shook his head. "None. Could it be a ruptured appendix?"

"No, you would have called an ambulance by now if it was," she said. The doctor removed the blood pressure monitor from his arm and grabbed a stethoscope. "How are your bowel movements?"

"Same as always, I'm regular every morning. I've started trying to eat more wholemeal cereal, bread and pasta and such. My best mate's a dietician, he told me to clean up my diet a bit."

She gave a faint nod of approval, though didn't pass any comment. He felt the cold metal disc on his stomach as she moved the stethoscope around and saw her forehead crease.

"What is it? Have you found something?" he said.

She kept the stethoscope focused to the right side of his bellybutton, moving it an inch or so this way and that way, up and down. The doctor said nothing as she removed the stethoscope and put on rubber gloves, though her face remained clouded.

Matthew swallowed. His throat felt dry. Why wasn't she saying anything? Her sudden silence worried him more than if she hadn't been loquacious in the first place.

The doctor began pressing his stomach with both hands, her fingertips prodding all over the dome of his bulging midriff. "Does it hurt when I push here?"

He winced. "Yes, it hurts like a bitch. Sorry."

She ignored the profanity. "Any pain here?"

The doctor touched further up, near his diaphragm. "No, just a dull discomfort," he answered.

Her hands jumped back down towards his appendix. "How about now?"

As she pushed, he watched in horror as his stomach seemed to crest like a wave on a choppy sea. His gut became deformed, no longer a round dome, but one with a distinct peak towards the right side. The curved peak pushed towards the middle and blinding pain seared through his torso. He screamed and threw his head back, arching his back and drawing his knees towards his stomach in the process.

Throbbing waves radiated throughout his body as he lay on his left side in spasms of agony. He growled outwards, then sucked in rattling breaths, then growled to expel more air in a never-ending futile cycle of trying to control the agony. What was happening to his body?

It looked like a parasite was in there; could a giant tapeworm be swimming in his abdomen? An image of a chest burster, like in *Aliens*, added to his terror. It didn't help that the nurse had turned the colour of wallpaper paste and stood, with both arms hanging at her sides, either in shock or dumbfounded as to what to do.

"Help! Please. Morphine," he cried.

"I'm going to book you in for an immediate scan. I'm going to fax this across to the hospital right away so that they see you as a matter of urgency."

***

Matthew stared at the ceiling of the ambulance as it ferried him to hospital; whether the Mater on the Crumlin Road, nearest to his house, or to the Royal in the middle of Belfast; he'd find out later. His head swam from the unceasing waves of pain radiating out from his abdomen, engulfing his entire nervous system.

Sonya was in the ambulance with him. Occasional flashes of orange hair passed before his eyes as she swooped down on him, leaning close to wipe his brow, or hold his hand. His body buffeted from side to side on the gurney and his head rolled from left cheek to right cheek, his eyes flickering towards the back of their respective sockets.

The sound of a siren. Oh no; he wanted to get to hospital on the double, not get pulled over to allow an emergency vehicle past. Oh wait; he *was* the emergency, in the vehicle and all. Onwards to treatment.

The whoosh of automatic doors opening, voices all around. The smell of smoke from patients outside the hospital, the smell of bleach inside. Bright lights from florescent tubes overhead, beeping sounds, rows of green-backed chairs like in a cinema, only this wasn't any fun. No fun at all. Patients waiting with no popcorn, no snacks, no movie to watch. Only a TV showing news, no doubt. More grim news from the world. Grim news for him to come from his internal world. What the hell was inside his body?

Matthew groaned and thrashed as another wave of pain smashed through even the dihydrocodeine almost sobering him completely.

He was wheeled into a room, prodded and manhandled, flipped and turned like a piece of meat by a spatula. Stomach bared, cold wet liquid applied on his torso. A plastic stick touched down on his gut; here, there everywhere. Attached to a cord. An ultrasound?

A high-pitched voice, the words a squeak. "Am I pregnant? Who got me knocked up, then?"

Whose words? His words? Giddy with laughter, not sounding like himself at all. Too high-pitched? His voice an octave higher like listening to himself in a video or MP3, an electronically filtered recording of himself. Was it the pain making him sing soprano?

Maybe he had a tapeworm in his gut. A parasite, not living in symbiosis, but leeching the life essence out of him. Get it out. Drag it out, proglottid by proglottid and stamp on it, until it was flat on the ground.

"Keep your chitinous hooks to yourself, you vermin!"

Again with the helium voice. No wait: it was himself again in that high-pitched voice. So be it. He was resigned to the fact that his voice had regressed to that of a prepubescent boy, not broken yet.

"There is a large, ill-defined heterogenous mass in the right side of the abdominal cavity having multiple hypoechoic areas and echogenic structures with internal vascularity present."

Who spoke? The sonographer? Talking to who? Not him, nor Sonya. A radiographer? Too science-y, too technical-y. Hypoechoic. Echogenic. Such big words, right over the head.

"Echo," he called. "Echo! Somebody explain why there is an echo. Have I got no organs?"

Plastic stick gone, paper rolls applied and wiping his stomach clear of gel.

"The scan showed a foreign object in your abdominal cavity. We're going to prep you for surgery, Mr. Savage."

"But this isn't my doctor's surgery," he said, drool running on his chin.

"No, I said we're taking you for an operation. Are you able to understand?"

A pause. Then the same voice, addressing someone else.

"What medicine was he given? He doesn't seem coherent."

"Co-codamol? I wasn't give any."

"Miss Parker, does your partner speak English as a first language?"

Sonya's exasperated voice. "Yes, of course he does, he's from here."

"We're going to take him for surgery, even though he doesn't seem able to give his consent. He hasn't signed a DNACPR."

Her confused voice. "What does that mean?"

"Do not resuscitate order. He needs immediate surgery or he's at risk of internal bleeding, maybe even sepsis."

Her voice again, now shocked. "What? Then, do what you have to do – if it's as bad as all that."

He echoed her sentiment, glad she could speak for him. She had come through for him when he needed her most. Like an angel in the darkness, she had flown in from whatever corner of heaven she'd been in, to rescue him. He had been wrong about her.

CHAPTER EIGHT

Seven. Lucky seven. Seven oh eight.

Seven hundred and eight. Seven oh eight. Seven hundred and eight – what?

Seven. Seven was a lucky number, right?

But seven oh eight was unlucky. Seven hundred and eight was unlucky. Bad luck. An unlucky omen. An omen of death.

Where did the number come from? It swirled in Matthew's head, flooding there on a tide of dihydrocodeine, carried by a tapeworm, breaking three proglottids into his bloodstream. As each one fell: first seven, then zero, then eight, they transmitted sepsis on a poisonous wave infiltrating his blood with bacteria.

He was dying. Such strange thoughts were the last gasps of his brain as it snuffed itself out.

Or not. He was still able to think complex thoughts. Like worrying about the number 708 and tapeworms, and sepsis.

"It is ready."

A woman's voice, in his ear, as though she were close to him. But, not in his ear. In his inner ear. In his head.

"Will it work?"

A man's voice, a deep baritone.

A witch and a soldier, speaking.

"It has already worked. It is done. By the Grace of the Lunar Goddess."

"I don't believe in magic of the moon, or of goddesses – or you. Prove it to me."

Defiance. He risked getting himself killed with those words. He didn't know how dangerous she was.

The hospital faded and he saw before his eyes an image of them both: witch and soldier. They were in her shabby hovel again. Her brown hair wasn't shaggy and matted as before, but hanging in long, neat spirals over her shoulders. She wore a linen tunic top that had a simple leather lace threaded through to fasten it across the bust; He noticed she had left it unfastened at the top, exposing the curve of her left breast. He peeled his eyes from her chest to the soldier. The soldier seemed to have noticed the same thing as he did, for his eyes drifted upwards from her ample chest to her face.

"I have other charms – apart from the obvious ones – that I've used to guarantee success," she teased.

The soldier threw her down on her thin, hay mattress and they had rough sex, a flurry of flying clothes and roving hands. It made him feel like an unwilling voyeur; he couldn't have peeled his eyes away if he'd wanted to, seeing as he was using his inner sight to witness scenes from a time long ago. How long ago? Seven hundred years ago.

Seven hundred and eight years ago.

In the year of Our Lord, thirteen hundred and fifteen. Seven hundred and eight years before the present day.

Soldier and witch fell apart, sweaty and panting. A sting of jealousy seized him as he watched them lying satisfied in post-coital bliss. Stomach pain and the physical barrier caused by the large girth of his midsection had put a dampener on carnal joys with Sonya of late – aside from their arguments over his health, money and, anything really. He glowered as he watched the muscular physique of the soldier as the man rose naked from the witch's humble straw bed.

"Let me see the urn."

The witch rose naked and handed a small, dyed purple, linen bag to him. He loosened the leather thong and reached inside. The soldier held it in his fingertips and inspected it, his eyes narrowed as he absorbed every detail of the intricate runes she had etched using a stylus, as he memorised each linear mark and curved design.

"It's certainly an impressive piece of craft. You guarantee it will work?"

She nodded. "Life blood has been poured into that. There is no doubt that success will follow."

"Last time I came here you told me my garrison would take Carraig Fhearghais Castle within this year.

49

On your word, we are camped outside, surrounding the twin towers of the gatehouse."

"You have my word that you will take it within the year," she said, a tad too quick, with dangerous defiance.

"But you also said the journey for my own personal success will take much longer and that I will die in my quest for glory."

"As you will, in victorious battle," she said, her voice low and menacing.

The soldier's lip curled. "Then how is that the beginning of my journey? You also told me before that it would mark the beginning, not end of my journey. I can't make sense of that."

"Because you are thinking in terms of one lifetime." She pinched the taut, naked skin of his sculpted torso. "As pleasurable as this is to the eye, the flesh is only a husk for the soul within. Flesh lasts one lifetime then goes back to the dust. But what happens to the soul?"

He blinked at her, a brooding silence filling her shabby hovel. "It goes to heaven. Or to hell. Hell for mine, after committing myself to this pagan magic and witchcraft, resigning myself to ungodly necromancy in the name of glory."

The witch pointed to a triangular rune on the blood-infused clay urn. It looked to Matthew's untrained eye as a less-than sign in mathematics.

"This symbol represents death. A great malady will afflict your tormented soul."

The soldier sneered but said nothing as she spoke.

"Aside from its symbolism, it also holds special meaning in numerology. It is the number seven."

Matthew rotated his spiritual mind's eye to the right and looked at the less-than sign sideways. Indeed, it resembled a number seven.

"Seven is the number of spiritual awakenment and the ability of the inner eye. Your enemy will harbour a negative bond towards you and the number seven will allow you to be free of this bond."

The witch turned the urn a fraction and pointed to a second rune. It looked like a capital letter D.

"This symbol represents danger and anguish. Your departure from this world will not be an easy one."

His heart wrenched at the distraught look on the soldier's face. The man wiped his expression clear a second later, as only a soldier, accustomed with death would do.

"In numerology, it is also representative of the energy of Sin, great God of the Moon, and marks the start of a spiritual journey. Yours will be a massive undertaking. Because it is the start of a journey, it presents as zero, or nought, a beginning."

He looked again at the second, D-shaped rune. It did depict a number zero; or as close a match as he could think of, in terms of a runic symbol.

The witch pointed to a third rune on the reverse side of the urn. It resembled an uppercase letter B if written in straight lines, appearing as two conjoined triangles, the peak of each appearing to the left.

"This symbol represents birth and liberation of the soul. Your murdered soul will be freed from its former prison."

"I will go to heaven?" said the soldier, his voice awash with relief.

She shook her head. "You will await your time to exact revenge on earth."

Revenge. On who? The people of Carrickfergus? The soldier was the one who had wronged the townspeople, not the other way around. He watched the soldier for his response.

"In numerology, this equates to the number eight. Eight represents the reciprocal tides as governed by the moon, which states that as you give so you shall receive."

"You reap what you sow," the soldier added, his voice bitter.

"Yes," she said with a smile.

Matthew studied the rune shaped like a linear, uppercase letter B. It did indeed resemble a number eight.

"For seven hundred and eight years, you will wait for your time to return to exact revenge. The time will come and all will be yours."

Seven hundred and eight years.

From medieval to present.

From thirteen fifteen to twenty twenty-three.

CHAPTER NINE

"Patient has reported pain in the lower retroperitoneum area. Morphine has been administered by intravenous."

A swarm of giant, green geese, flocking all around. One, two, three, a gaggle, half a dozen, a score, all having a gander at his naked torso. Naked yellow torso, smeared with apple sauce. He should be eating the geese, not them eating him.

"Exploratory laparotomy confirms the radiological imaging and preoperative diagnosis from the CT."

"Not suspected to be a teratoma."

"Suspected FIF to be removed by surgical excision."

Teratoma. Not a goose, a turtle, a terrapin. A terrapin turtle tickling his tummy.

Matthew laughed and his head lolled, heavy as a lump of clay.

CT. So that had been a scan, when they had slathered all the wet, gooey stuff all over his gut. So what was FIF?

"Fif," he slurred. "Fucked if I know, that's what it stands for. Should be FIKK, not FIF."

A strange sensation: a tugging, pulling, like a fishing hook and line were attached to the skin on his lower belly.

"Heterogenous mass in the lower right quadrant of the retroperitoneum as identified in the scan is now confirmed as a FIF, removed by surgical excision."

Had he been asleep? Knocked out by morphine? If so, then why was he now awake? He was woozy, everything heavy and spinning. Next, he was on a distant planet; one with high gravity. Now he was stuck to the gurney. The large circular light above dazzled his eyes and he peeled them away from it, letting his gaze sweep across the green-gowned geese all around, then down to his own foreign body. A red mass, a foreign object removed from his belly. A red, slippery, slimy grapefruit-sized flesh ball.

"What's that? Where did you get that?"

The robotic voice of a medic spoke. "Patient is awake. Administer a second dose and note the time at nineteen hundred and seven hours."

"I'm not in pain, don't knock me out again."

A notch more friendly, now directed at him. "Try not to speak, Mr. Savage."

He pointed at the grapefruit-sized fleshy mass. "Is that a tumour?"

The voice switched back to a robotic, impersonal one, dictating medical notes. "Mass is enclosed in a sac, appearing dark pink in colour, containing fat, malformed bony and cartilaginous tissue and serous fluid."

His finger shook as he pointed. "That thing didn't come out of me, did it?"

"Mass will be sent for histopathological examination to confirm analysis of the tissues."

"Erm, will somebody please explain to me what's happening? Was that a cancerous tumour in my body?"

Matthew felt himself rolled onto his left hip. He looked back over his right shoulder and saw a flash of a large syringe, which was placed in his lower back, before the world swam red, then white.

***

"Sonya? What day is it?"

Sonya jumped out of her chair like she'd sat on a pin. "You're awake. I'll get the doctor."

She came back a moment later followed by a tall, thin man wearing a shirt and tie, not a white coat, or scrubs of any sort. Maybe a surgeon or some other upper-up? The lack of medical attire gave him an air of importance, somehow.

"Matthew. How are you feeling?"

He smacked his dry lips together. "Thirsty."

The doctor pulled a wheely table closer, and he saw a jug of water and glass. "You've been sedated and sleeping for most of the past three days."

He took a sip of water. "Do I have bowel cancer?"

"No. There was no teratoma present. Nothing of malignant potential, fortunately."

Teratoma. He recalled the word being tossed around when one of the medics had been dictating the operation; or had that all been part of an elaborate dream he'd had?

"If it wasn't cancer, then why did I need surgery?"

A red ball. A grapefruit-sized flesh ball.

The doctor gave a bland smile and blinked; he imagined the man composing his thoughts into layman's terms for his benefit.

"There was a large mass inside your abdomen. It was removed and sent for histopathological examination – tests," said the doctor.

"What did the tests show?"

Sonya, behind the doctor, chewed her bottom lip and rubbed her arms as though cold, though he knew she did it to self-soothe.

"The mass had areas of tissues lined by respiratory epithelium, intestinal epithelium and stratified squamous epithelium. There was a malformed spinal column and structures resembling limb buds. The mass also had hair and the presence of three teeth."

"Hair? And teeth? Whose teeth?" By way of reflex, he ran his tongue across his top and bottom teeth: all were present. None had even been loosened from his jaw, never-mind knocked out.

"The organ tissues present were of a foreign body, Matthew. The mass we discovered inside you was known as a foetus-in-foetu."

Foetus-in-foetu: FIF. Not Fucked if I know, foetus-in-foetu.

"I know what a foetus is. But I'm a man. Are you saying I was pregnant? That's impossible."

The doctor shook his head. "You had normal levels of Human Chorionic Gonadotrophin in your body. HCG is the pregnancy hormone, present in women who have ectopic pregnancies, where an embryo begins to grow outside of the uterus. In your case, you had a foetus-in-foetu."

"It was your twin, Matthew." Sonya's voice cracked; she could have done with a sip of water herself.

The doctor gave a faint nod in agreement with her. "When you were conceived, there was another egg. That embryo would have developed into your brother, but at some point during your mother's pregnancy, you became the dominant twin and absorbed the other zygote. It then continued to develop inside you, taking its blood supply from your abdominal wall plexus."

Matthew felt sick. Sick, but hollow at the same time. Empty. He lowered his hands to his stomach and cupped them over his bandaged gut. Even clad in medical fabric, it looked a great deal smaller than it had been his whole life.

He looked at Sonya. "See? I wasn't fat at all."

She offered a faint smile, though she looked the colour of wallpaper paste.

He turned back to the doctor. "Where is the mass of tissue now?"

"It has been removed for disposal in the medical waste facility. Why? Is there a reason you ask?"

"Could he have it for burial, maybe?" Sonya's hopeful face flitted from the doctor, to Matthew, and back to the doctor again. She was trying to read his mind. Wrong, nonetheless, though he appreciated it all the same.

The doctor's eyebrows arched high above the frame of his glasses. "Is that what you would like to do, Matthew?"

He sniffed. "No. I have no particular reason to want to cremate my parasitic twin."

The last two words had barely left his mouth when a large shudder overcame his body. Parasitic twin. A brother that he had never known about; one who had leeched his life force from him for the past thirty-three years.

"When will he be able to come home?" she said.

"If the postoperative period continues to be uneventful, you can go home in another two days' time, Mr. Savage." The doctor offered a playful smile in Sonya's direction. "I'll discharge you into good hands, if that is the case."

She rewarded the doctor's smile with a batting of her eyelids. Matthew rolled his eyes. Could've been worse; at least they weren't playing tonsil tennis over his dead body.

The doctor swept out of the room, leaving them in an awkward silence. He forced his eyes across to meet hers over his hospital bed.

"You must think I'm a mutant. I suppose I am. A genetic one, in any case," he said, his tone morose.

She perched on the edge of his bed and cupped his left hand in both of hers. "No, babe, not at all. I'd never think something like that. It could've happened to anyone."

He guffawed. "I'm sure that isn't actually true, but I appreciate the effort. I'll bet having a parasitic twin is more like one in a million."

She released his hand and reached for her phone, her spidery fingers scuttling over the screen. "One in five hundred thousand, as a matter of fact. Not far wrong."

He let his chin drop onto his chest, his downcast eyes on the sea of bandages wrapped around his middle. "You should go and find yourself a real man, a better one with a good body who can actually hold down a job without taking sick days all the time. Oh, and not a freak."

She gave a weak smile. "Such a fella doesn't exist. But I appreciate you giving me your blessing to find myself a fantasy man. I'll head on down the pub and look for one then while you're laying in bed here then, eh?"

He opened his mouth to argue, before realising she was joking. Maybe he'd got her all wrong. After twelve years together, did he know her? Did he know himself?

CHAPTER TEN

A FUB. A fat, useless bastard. That's what the lads at work called him anyway; but not anymore. Starting today he was slimline Matt. Not fatty Matty, not now or evermore. No FIF and no FUB.

Matthew drummed his fingers on the bandages enclosing his girth. His midriff still resembled an Egyptian mummy. Wonder what his new physique would look like without the bulging mass making it appear distorted? He didn't go to the gym regularly enough to have sculpted abs, but maybe he'd actually have a flat abdomen, rather than a rounded, barrel-shaped torso. A tremor of excitement seized him; it might even do wonders for his sex life with Sonya.

Speaking of Sonya, where the hell had she been for the past two days while he'd been lying in bed, his brain dissolving under the mind-numbing influence of daytime TV? Yes, she had work during the day on the excavation in Carrickfergus, and without him to drop her off, she was no doubt having to carpool it to work. Still, that didn't explain her lack of visits for the past two evenings. Visitors were allowed in the wards until eleven, the hospital staff had said. But she hadn't turned up, even once, in the past couple of days.

He grabbed his phone off the wheely hospital table where the remnants of his half-eaten dinner remained. *Hey sugar, where u at, don't you want to see ur hot n sexy new boyfriend? Didn't even need the gym either, lol.*

Send.

No response. Usually she replied within minutes. She was always on her phone.

His idle fingers drifted to a cursory search for foetus-in-foetu. Why was he torturing himself? Morbid curiosity? No: education was the best equipment for life.

"Foetus-in-foetu is usually retro – perry." A pause as he read aloud. Damn medical terminology, too hard to pronounce. "Retro-peri-to-neal but there have been cases reported in other areas such as the cranial cavity and scrotal sac. Ugh!"

He dropped the phone onto the bed as though it were full of germs. Having a parasitic twin in the brain was bad enough, but one in the balls? It made him shudder. He imagined a grapefruit-sized testicle and clenched his legs together.

The things that boredom made him do. He sighed and glanced once more at his phone. A notification popped up; finally a reply from Sonya. *Soz babe, was held up in traffic, Tony dropped me off, be inside in a mo.*

What time was it anyway? Quarter past six. There was no way traffic was that bad to hold them up so long; the archaeological dig was a nine to five job and Carrickfergus to Belfast was a half hour drive going against the rush hour traffic. Furthermore, if they were stuck in traffic with Tony driving, and Sonya sitting in the passenger side, then surely she would have had ample time to reply to one quick text? His mind worked overtime as he stared at their texts but came up with no explanations.

The door to his private room opened and she swept in, her red fringe parted in curtains and a pink flush across her cheeks, scarf askew around her neck.

"Was traffic bad yesterday evening too?" Passive aggressive, perhaps, but he couldn't pass up the opportunity to needle her about her lack of visit the day before either.

She threw cow-eyes at him. "No, you'll never believe what happened. Jessie escaped."

Jessie, of course, her pampered house cat. A likely excuse.

"Did you find her?"

She tucked a stray red strand behind her right ear and sat down in the visitor's chair next to his bed. "Yes, eventually. She'd got herself stuck up high in the neighbour's tree. Something must have spooked her, it's not like Jessie to take off."

"I didn't know Jessie could climb," he snorted.

"Don't make fun of her." She stuck her bottom lip out in faux offence. "She was really frightened, she was hissing. It took her ages to come to me, I had to tempt her with a can of Spam, it's all there was in the house."

Also typical. No food in the cupboards.

"Well, I'm sure she'll get over it with a bit of therapy," he said.

She glared at him. "You're salty tonight. Is it because I didn't visit?"

"You didn't even text or call. Was Jessie so important that you couldn't have even got in touch, even to ask how I'm doing?" His voice sounded whiny in his own ears; like a petulant teenage boy. He took a deep breath. "Sorry, sugar. I'm just struggling to process the operation and the fact that I've had an alien living inside me since before I was born. It's a lot to get my head round."

"Exactly – I thought a bit of head space would've done you some good to think it all over."

He lowered his chin and looked down at the bandages on his gut.

"Ack, babe, don't be like that." She put a finger on his chin and lifted it, turning his face towards hers. "I'll make it up to you. Look what I brought."

She brought a foot long Subway sandwich out of her bag.

"Smells fantastic after all the hospital food. Did you bring me a beer to wash it down?" He winked at her, and she grinned. What a feat; smoothing things over between them was a rare feat these days.

"So, anyway, what was causing the bad traffic tonight?"

The flush brightened on her cheeks. "Um, there was tailback from an accident on the M2, I think. I didn't see it though, just the emergency vehicles."

"Of course. You mustn't have got any reception all the way out there in Carrickfergus either, seeing as you didn't get my text right away." He was being a complete dick and he knew it; but something didn't add up about her excuses. Something was off. A gut feeling, maybe, but he knew it.

"Aww, you caught me out. I'm having an affair, there, I said it." Her eyes were bright with a cheeky, taunting energy, an impish grin on her face. "It's with Tony. No, better still, it's with a mystery man who you don't even know about. Didn't you say you wanted me to find a fantasy fella?"

He raised his eyebrows in mock-curiosity. "Oh, I see. Naturally, I should have known that all along then."

"Well, it's what you were thinking, Sherlock, with all your line of questioning?" She winked at him in the same way he'd done to her before.

He bit into his Subway and let silence fall between them. Jokes with a jag, back and forth, verbal tennis. Was he even good for her? Was she good for him? They always seemed to nag each other, or snipe at each other. Was that a healthy way to be? Maybe not the best. Self-improvement: he would work on being a better person and try to be nicer towards her in the process. They had been together for twelve years, their relationship deserved that much respect at least. No; they deserved to respect themselves – and each other.

It was a good note to end his train of thought on; but his brain wouldn't be stopped. Could she be giving him a double bluff; what if she really was having an affair? She hadn't given him any indication before that she was seeing someone else; but now she had stuck the idea in his head. A metaphorical parasitic twin had been implanted, its stem cells spreading and growing, letting its paranoid ideas take root in his mind.

CHAPTER ELEVEN

Matthew stretched out across the sofa, a saucer with a sandwich balanced on his stomach. His gut was much flatter now, though still misshapen, with some loose skin under his belly button. After he had first removed the bandages, he had stood staring at his abdomen for an hour in the hallway mirror; front facing, then sideways to the left and sideways to the right. He didn't recognise himself in the mirror. His physique looked completely different to how he had ever known it. Now, instead of looking lumpy and barrel-shaped, he looked like a deflated balloon. The sagging skin gave the impression that he had lost a lot of weight.

Technically that was true, though he had lost the weight of his parasitic twin, rather than fat loss – even though his outward appearance suggested he had once been obese.

He wasn't a slim man by any means, though his medium-build torso now matched his slim arms and legs. The saggy skin would take some getting used to, though he was happy to be pain-free, so appearance was of lesser importance. Granted, he looked forward to a shopping trip to get some smaller sized shirts and t-shirts now that he didn't need XXL sizes as he didn't have any misshapen bulk to hide.

Miaow. The cat calling for attention interrupted his thoughts.

"What do you want, Jessie? You looking for some food? I thought Sonya fed you before she left for work." He opened his sandwich and pulled out some of the ham. "That'll have to do you, I'm afraid. I need to rest so my stitches will heal."

Jessie ate the ham that he chucked on the hardwood floor. She licked her face and raised her head to him with another miaow.

"Can't you go on outside and catch a mouse, or a bird? You're the fattest one in this family now that I've lost my bulk." He patted his stomach and winced; still sore. He'd have to remember not to do that anymore.

The cat answered with another Miaow.

"Oh, come on, Jessie. Look at me." He pointed to his stitches. "I look like I've just had a fecking caesarean. Now I know what new mums must feel like. I'll bet you wouldn't be so hard on Sonya if it were her lying here, not me."

Miaow.

The pampered moggie wasn't going to let him off the hook. He set his lunch on the coffee table then rolled off the sofa, keeping his stomach as flat as possible, as he landed on all fours and pushed himself upright, using the sofa for balance. Bending hurt, and he was paranoid about ripping the stitches if he moved his torso too much.

"There now, you silly cat. Come on, I'll find you some nibbles in the kitchen and then you can go outside and get out of my hair for a bit."

As he led the way into the kitchen, a shadow passing outside the window caught his eye. Was someone in the back garden? With thoughts of Jessie's snack abandoned, he traipsed to the back door, unlocked it and peered outside.

Nobody. Very odd. He could've sworn he saw the shadow of a man flash past the window.

A tickle at his ankles announced Jessie's presence between his feet. The cat arched her back, her fur standing upright, and hissed. He looked down at her, bewildered. She continued to hiss and stare out the door into the garden.

"I'm not the only one who thinks something odd is going on then, it seems, huh?" He locked the kitchen door, then opened the last tin of cat meat in the cupboard.

As he passed out of the kitchen, he caught sight of the mirror in the hallway. It reflected the front door, from the angle where he stopped, as he turned into the living room. For a split second, a man's face had appeared reflected in the mirror from outside. The reflection had been distorted because of the opaque windowpane in the front door, but he had distinguished enough to see that the man had black hair and a black beard, much like his own.

Somebody had to be out there. He strode along the hallway and pulled the front door open.

Nobody.

"Hello?" He walked down the short garden path and peered over the gate, looking left, then right. The street was empty.

Very odd. He turned back up his garden path, but instead of going back inside, he continued around the side path into the back garden. Once he was sure that the back garden had no intruders and the front garden and street beyond were clear, he went back inside.

Very, very odd. He shook his head to himself. Not to worry; maybe he was simply preoccupied with his operation and was feeling jumpy as a result of being alone, so had imagined someone else being there.

Back to the living room. Jessie was sitting on the windowsill overlooking the front garden, her teeth bared as she hissed, her face inclined outside.

"Stop it, would you Jessie? You're not helping my goosebumps." He lifted her off the windowsill and dropped her onto the floor. The cat stalked out of the room. Did she give him a disapproving look as she passed? Probably.

"Hey babe."

Sonya's unexpected voice caused him to jump and cry out. She laughed and clapped her hands over her mouth. "Oh, my goodness, I didn't mean to scare the crap out of you. I thought I'd surprise you as I got back a bit early. What's got you so spooked?"

He shook his head. "Just being by myself, I think. I don't like being left alone with my thoughts."

"Did you get any sleep at all?"

"No, I don't like taking naps, it stops me falling asleep later."

She set her soil-coated backpack down by the living room door and unzipped it. "I brought you something from the dig to cheer you up. You're going to love this."

It was a polythene bag. Inside the clear plastic, he saw what looked like a maroon-coloured sphere the size of a grapefruit. For one horrible moment, he thought she had brought home the foetus-in-foetu and gagged; until she turned it over and he saw that he had been looking at the underside of a small clay pot. Sonya extracted it with a delicate grip and cupped it in both palms. The circular object was covered everywhere except the base in intricate linear markings.

Runes.

His stomach jolted as though on a rollercoaster. It was the pot from his dreams, the one the witch had made from clay and the blood of a Scottish soldier.

"Where did you get that?" he said, his voice shaky.

"I found it on the spoil heap at the dig today. Anything on the spoil heap is of no use as it isn't found in situ, so I brought it home. It's a present for you." She offered the pot to him.

He didn't take it, though couldn't peel his eyes away from it. "Are you allowed to do that? You've never brought any other artefacts home before."

"I know." She cocked her head in a nonchalant manner. "But this one called to me. I felt a connection to it, like it was sending me a vibe to take it. I wouldn't have found it if it wasn't for the funny feeling I had."

"What funny feeling?" His voice continued to waver.

"Just that there was something behind me, like a person standing there. When I turned, there was nobody of course, but then I saw it peeking out of the spoil heap. It's lovely, don't you think?"

"It's cursed. It's evil."

Her face crumpled. "A fat lot of thanks that is, I thought you would love it."

"It's the pot from my dream, the one the witch used. She mixed the clay with the blood of a Scottish soldier and said an incantation to make them win – the garrison attacking Carrickfergus town."

She hugged the clay pot against her left shoulder and turned her back a fraction, in a protective gesture. "Well, if you don't want it, then don't take it. I'll keep it for myself. I just thought, seeing as how worried you were about me being home late the past few nights that I'd come home early for a change and bring you something nice."

He let the logical part of his brain override his fears. "Listen, I'm sorry, sugar. I don't mean to be ungrateful. I know I'm highly strung at the moment. I'm a barrel of insecurity and worry – and I'm sure I'm a pain in the arse. I hope I show you how much I love and appreciate you, and all you do for me."

Sonya's taut expression melted into a smile. "It's alright babe, I understand. I'll put the pot on the fireplace, and you can have it if you want, but if not, it can be a nice decorative piece for us all to enjoy."

She set the pot on the mantel above the electric fire. He turned away from it with a shudder.

CHAPTER TWELVE

The public entry floor of the Keep at Carraig Fhearghais Castle was dingy, as there were no windows. To make it worse, all the candles had burned low in their holders, causing the whitewashed walls to look grey. A rank smell pervaded the air. It was a mixture of blood, sweat, and urine, but mostly of death. Flecks of flesh from the enemy clung to the soldiers' chausses and mail. Seven foot-soldiers awaited news from the scouts. They were busy drawing water from the deep well in the middle of the room, filling pail upon pail and ferrying them out. Boiling water was needed for the gatehouse, ready to pour upon the

Scottish enemy, if they persisted in trying to attack the castle, as they had burned the town.

The last day of May stood in stark contrast to the first. The Beltaine festival on the 1st day of the month had seen feasting and merriment. Fires had been lit to welcome in the start of summer. How sad that on the 26th of May, the fires that had been lit were by the Scottish enemy, to burn and loot Carraig Fhearghais town, not celebrate. Now, on the 31st of May, mere days after the invasion had started, the foot-soldiers and men-at-war who defended the castle under Henry Thrapston, Keeper of Carraig Fhearghais Castle, were tired and on edge after four days of fighting, with barely any rest or time to eat.

They had lost many good men when the Scottish garrison had launched a surprise attack on the town and now the remaining number of Thrapston's men, whittled down to fifty, were holed up inside the castle.

While the seven foot-soldiers filled pails of water and awaited Thrapston's word, the remainder of the fifty defended the castle; archers lined the towers, while others waited with stones at the gatehouse machicolations, or were ready to pour boiling water through the murder-hole.

The Keeper descended the winding stairwell from the middle floor, the chamber for the Lord's entourage. Like his men, he wore mail and a red surcoat, emblazoned with a yellow cross with the red hand of Ulster in the centre; a blood-red right hand with its palm facing forwards and fingers aligned upwards. These were the colours of Richard de Burgh, the Red Earl of Ulster.

One of the soldiers stopped filling his pail and watched Thrapston, eager for news. He had removed his nasal-helm and padded arming cap before he had begun the repetitive task of drawing water, though he remained in his mail and red surcoat with the Red Earl's crest, ready for battle. The weight of his armour, weighing at least two sacks full of groats, dragged on his exhausted body that was desperate for food and rest.

Aymer. The soldier's name was Aymer. How did he know this? He looked down his own body, then touched his own face with calloused, fingertips.

Because he wasn't Matthew. He was a medieval soldier: Aymer.

Was this a dream? If it was, it was a lucid one.

"I bring bad tidings. Edward Bruce has had himself inaugurated as High King of all Ireland," said Thrapston. "They say he did this without the word of the Red Earl."

"What of the Grand Coalition? What happened to the Celtic Alliance? The Bruce promised us that much," said Aymer.

"King Robert the Bruce promised us that, not Edward, in the name of our common ancestry and customs," said the Keeper.

"But Edward is his brother. We invited him here ourselves. It's written there, in the Chronicle of John of Tynemouth – you read it to us only last year that the brother of King Robert, aspiring to Kingship in Ireland, had gathered together an army to come to Ireland with the support of the Irish, in the name of a Celtic Alliance," said another of the seven soldiers.

"That much is true, but he said that during his Irish campaigns, we have proved unreliable partners in any coalition," said the Keeper.

"The only thing unreliable was his good word. He was far too ambitious, we should have known this much from the start that all he wanted was to become King of Ireland and exploit our food resources, diverting our exports away from Carlisle to send to Scotland," said another soldier.

Henry Thrapston took a deep breath and exhaled, long and slow. "The Scots have more men. Edward landed 6000 men at Latharna, sailing 300 galleys across from Ayr. He attacked us here while his brother, King Robert attacked Carlisle. Our scouts send word that Northburgh has already fallen. It is only a matter of time before Greencastle falls too. Then we will be isolated – if they can control Carraig Fhearghais Castle, they control the North passage."

"The castle will not fall." A soldier next to Aymer raised an angry fist, his mitten dangling from the hauberk as he punched the air in outrage. "We will not have to surrender, we will be relieved before this year is out."

A cry of agreement sounded among the seven. Aymer remained silent in thought.

"This castle is impregnable. No one can breach these walls," said Aymer.

"Yes, and we have enough provisions. Thirty crannocks of wheat will be on their way to us soon. The famine that ravages our land will not see us perish, nor will the Scots. We will hold out. We will fight," said another.

The rousing cry was louder, three among the seven soldiers punching the air.

"I say we never surrender, regardless of whether we are relieved or not," Aymer added.

Two more soldiers shouted their support of his words.

The Keeper pressed his lips together in firm resolve. "We need support. Many of the Irish Chieftains have already joined the Scots. They were betrayed by a lie. There is no Celtic alliance. We are in an untenable position."

Aymer raised his chin in defiance at such a defeatist stance by the Keeper. "Then what would you have us do? I for one will fight back, always. We will take prisoners — the gatehouse is empty, as are the small towers of the Middle Ward and the Oubliette. We fight back — always. No surrender."

CHAPTER THIRTEEN

"Matthew? Matthew, are you alright?"

He blinked a few times in rapid succession, finding that his eyes were bone dry. His ears were still full of the rallying cries of soldiers from a past era, seven hundred years ago.

"I lost you there, for a moment."

The psychologist's face drifted in and out of focus, and he let his gaze settle on the blue, plastic rim of her glasses. Her eyes, magnified behind the lenses, were worried.

"Are you okay? Do you need to step out for air?"

"I – I," he started. He wiped his hair off his clammy forehead. "I don't know what happened, I blanked out. What was I saying?"

He looked around her room, regaining his orientation. He was in the hospital, seeing the counsellor that his doctor had contacted as a follow up to his surgical procedure. Matthew rubbed his eyes and took a sip of water from the glass on the small circular table in front.

"You were telling me about the strange dreams you'd been having – of a witch and a Scottish soldier – and then you'd just gone on to talk about a pot that your girlfriend brought back from her archaeological dig in Carrickfergus when you stopped talking and went slack."

"I had another vision," he said, in between gasps.

"You mean, a dream," she corrected.

He shook his head, dislodging hair that was wet with sweat across his forehead. "No, that's not it. It was a vision. I'm sure of it now – what I've been seeing was real. It really happened, seven hundred years ago. This time I didn't see the Scottish soldier or the witch. I was among the Anglo-Irish garrison inside Carrickfergus. I was a soldier called Aymer."

The psychologist's mouth twitched as though she were about to smile but refrained from doing so. "I think that having surgery, and the loss of a part of you, something you carried for thirty-three years, has been very hard on you."

"No, that's not it." He waved his hands, not caring how petulant that made him seem. "Something has been happening. I'm being shown details of a past conspiracy between a local Anglo-Irish witch and a Scottish soldier in Edward Bruce's army. There's another man involved now, a third man, who was one of the Carrick soldiers. I need to find out why my brain is telling me this information – and more to the point, what I'm expected to do with it."

"What happened seven hundred years ago is history. It's nothing to do with today. I'm concerned about your frame of mind at the moment, Matthew, and not without good cause. Surgery has a big impact not only on one's physical health, but on the mental health too." Her voice was calm, her eyes pleading.

He sighed. It was futile to argue with her; she was a hospital appointed psychologist with a job to do. That job was to ensure that he was medically fit – both mentally and physically – and then he could truly be discharged, without having cause to bring a lawsuit against the hospital. He ground his teeth and held his tongue from arguing.

"That thing that came out of me was more like a tumour than a person. It's weird to think of it as my–" He paused, feeling the revulsion of the next words. "Parasitic twin. I mean, it was just a grapefruit-sized ball of cells."

"It had functioning bodily tissues and bones. I read the medical notes. Your brother's blood supply was connected to your abdominal wall plexus. It was more than a tumorous ball of cells," she said.

He gave an involuntary shiver. "It's gone now, thank goodness. It was nothing more than a burden, and for the past month, a painful one at that."

"But it's something that your head needs space to grieve properly, regardless of whether you saw it as a person, or a ball of cells. Have you thought about a burial?"

He stared at her. "A what?"

"Holding a funeral for your brother – or for the part of yourself that was cut away and removed."

A nervous laugh escaped his diaphragm, high-pitched and riddled with fear.

"I'm very serious. I think it's exactly what you need to properly let go and be able to move on. Carrying a foetus-in-foetu with you since birth and now being separated can leave you, metaphorically speaking, empty. You need to properly address the void."

Void. Dark and dangerous things could fill a void. Like a malicious witch and a soldier, blinded by glory. "Void?" he said, his voice a croak.

She pursed her lips. "How does the idea of a funeral sound to you?"

"It's probably too late. I'm sure they dumped it in the medical waste. The surgery was last week. I really doubt they'd have kept it seven days later, even if they were running tests on the tissue," he said.

"Even if they don't have the remains, it might be good for you to hold a ritual to mark the passing of the foetus-in-foetu. But if you like, I could enquire for you?"

He nodded and lowered his eyes. As the psychologist left the room, he let his gaze settle on the rough, brown carpet though really, he was seeing nothing. Nothing except distracting thoughts of the past meandering through his head.

So far, in the several visions of the Scottish soldier and Anglo-Irish witch that he had witnessed, he didn't yet know either of their names. Not only that, but he had watched the scenes unfold as an outsider, like a ghost observing them. This latest vision had been different. He had actually been *inside* the body of the soldier inside Carrickfergus castle, and even knew the fella's name: Aymer. It gave the past an intimacy that none of his previous visions had. It was though he was more *personally* connected to Aymer, the Anglo-Irish soldier. He had seen everything through Aymer's eyes. It was as though he had actually *been* the soldier at Carrickfergus for a brief moment as he had witnessed the past.

How disturbing. Absorbed as he was by his thoughts, he jumped as the psychologist re-entered the room.

"I'm afraid I have bad news, Matthew. The remains have disappeared. There was no trace of them in the medical waste facility, nor any record of them having been there."

His stomach bottomed out. "Have they been taken away for tests – or medical research, maybe?"

"I don't think so – there would have been a record. It's as though they just, simply, disappeared," she said, her palms turned upwards.

CHAPTER FOURTEEN

He was a mutant. He was a freak. He was a man who had carried his unborn twin around in his abdomen since birth; a host for a parasitic foetus-in-foetu.

Was the pain – that stabbing, shocking pain that seemed to set all his neurones on fire – what women felt like if they suffered an ectopic pregnancy? One of Sonya's colleagues had once had an ectopic pregnancy, where the embryo had started growing in the fallopian tube, and she had needed the whole tube removed. His own surgery made him feel like nothing more than a walking incubator for another life that had leeched off his own body rather than nourishing it. Foetus-in-foetu. Didn't foetuses share stem cells with their mothers; cells that were known to help heal their bodies? Not so his own parasitic twin. It had stolen blood supply and nutrients from his body and had given him only an oversized unsightly torso and searing pain in return. Nothing symbiotic about that relationship; he was only too glad the mass had been removed from his body.

Matthew lifted the toilet seat up and ripped the paper off the packet. As he pulled the small, plastic applicator out of the packet, a wave of embarrassment swept over him. He was about to take a pregnancy test; not because he thought he was pregnant, but because he needed peace of mind. He needed to know if carrying the grossly overdeveloped embryo of his unborn twin brother around in his body for thirty-three years had elevated his levels of female hormones: human chorionic gonadotrophin, to be specific. HCG was the pregnancy hormone. What about his levels of progesterone, also associated with pregnancy? He glanced sideways at his reflection in the bathroom mirror. The pectoral muscles in his chest were covered by so much fat that he was sure the majority of the population would describe him as having man boobs. Could his man boobs be caused by three decades of his parasitic twin flooding his body with progesterone and HCG?

Nothing for it. He held the stick over the toilet and pissed on it. Easy for a man. How did women do it when they had nothing to aim with? Did they hold it under themselves, over the toilet bowl, and hose their own hand in the process? Sonya had never been pregnant, so there was no point in asking her.

His urine began to spread up the stick like a litmus paper. The stick reminded him of Covid lateral flow tests, only longer. He'd had Covid once, had seen the two lines appear on the screen. This time, he waited for two lines to appear, indicating that the levels of female hormones in his body were high enough as a result of his recently removed foetus-in-foetu twin.

One line appeared: negative.

So, HCG and progesterone weren't the cause of his moobs. Matthew sighed. Maybe the psychologist was right; he needed to take a proactive approach to dealing with stumbling blocks in his life.

Maybe he was just making excuses for excuses.

He threw the test in the pedal bin and slouched out of the bathroom. Thank goodness Sonya wasn't home, or she'd never let him live it down; the pregnancy jokes would last a lifetime. On second thought, better cover it up some more. He turned back into the bathroom and kicked the test to the bottom of the bin, then covered it with tissues and junk to hide from Sonya's *sleekit* eyes.

As he trudged down the hallway and into the living room, images from his latest vision filled his mind. In the scene from seven hundred years ago, he had embodied an Anglo-Irish soldier, Aymer, fighting for Carrickfergus. Such a contrast between their two lives; a bitter, metallic tang flooded Matthew's mouth as he acknowledged how strong and masculine the soldier had been, in comparison to his dumpy, foetus-infested self. He was a failure of a man: of a boyfriend; of a person, and he felt truly emasculated. Matthew hung his head as he flopped down onto the sofa for another day of dwelling in self-pity. Better make the most of it; his sick leave was due to end on Friday and then he'd be back to work, ready to take more verbal abuse about being a fat bastard, and any other insults-of-the-day from his horrible colleagues.

The image of Aymer faded and a new image popped into his mind: a dark red, grapefruit-sized mass. He recalled the green-gowned surgeon at the hospital holding the disgusting ball.

Now, he pictured it on a surgical tray, next to his hospital bed, while he lay immobile on the gurney. The flesh ball rolled around in small circles before centring itself. A soft, wet sound emanated from it and with disgust, Matthew saw that the flesh peeled back in two evenly spaced positions close to the centre of the mass. Underneath the peeled-back flesh were two brown eyeballs, looking directly at him. A gash lower down in the foetus-in-foetu appeared, forming a crude, misshapen mouth.

Intrusive thoughts. Nothing but his own brain being cruel to himself.

"Hello brother," it said, in a coarse version of his own voice.

His upper lip curled at the image in his mind. His mind sure could imagine the most disgusting things.

"Don't you have anything to say to me? You've always wanted a brother."

"Not like this." He answered inside his thoughts.

Across the room in the corner near the door, Jessie hissed and arched her back, teeth bared and fur standing on end as she faced him. The cat momentarily distracted him from the imagined aftermath of his parasitic twin brother in the hospital.

"I have what you want," his brother taunted.

"And what exactly is that?" Even in his mind, his voice dripped with disdain.

"Testosterone, for a start. I took it all. I leeched it from you and left you with those." The fleshy ball's eyes dropped from Matthew's face to his chest.

"Go away. Get out of my head. You have nothing useful to say." This time there was a hard edge to his voice; he spat each word, as though each were profane.

"Yes, I do and that's why you're thinking of me. I have all the things you want – and more."

In spite of himself, his interest was piqued. "Why don't you stop making cryptic fucking hints and get right to the point?"

"And there I was, going to ask you to grow a pair." The fleshy ball's eyes crinkled as it's wide, slit-like mouth smiled.

"I have the charisma that you don't, and the confidence too. I have the masculinity that you so badly desire. You want to win Sonya's affection back, but you don't know how. Well, I do."

"Oh, so now you think you can teach me something?" He scoffed.

"I know everything you know."

He waggled a finger at it. "No, you don't. What do you know? I've been around much longer than you. What could you possibly know more than me?"

"I know *more* than what you know, too. Don't forget, I was inside you listening to everything going on in the outside world and signals coming from inside you as well. Your fat gut was quite the amplifier, I must say."

It hadn't occurred to him that his parasitic twin might have been sentient, inside him, listening all that time; for three decades.

"The outside world and your *internal* world too."

A jolt of alarm seized him. "What do you mean by that? Are you talking about my thoughts? I don't believe for a minute that you were able to read my mind. That's not possible."

The gash of a smile twitched upwards at one corner, forming into a sneer. "Oh, but that's exactly what I'm talking about. I could see into your heart, Matthew. Into your soul."

Into your soul. The last three words were a hiss, a whisper, poured into his ear in a soothing venom.

His parasitic twin rolled off the surgical tray and slithered out of the operating theatre; it used dangling sinew and veins to pull itself, like tentacles, across the floor.

He shook his head to dislodge the horrible, imagined aftermath of what had really happened during his surgery. He smacked his temples several times, puffing and blowing in the process. "Get the fuck out of my head, you bastard, and stay out!"

With that, the menacing influence of his parasitic brother was gone.

"I saw the doctors cut you out of me, but that's it. Over. You didn't slither away, you weren't alive. My imagination did that just to torment me. They dumped you in medical waste." He spoke aloud, his words panicked in the empty living room.

The hospital psychologist, though. She had confirmed that it was missing.

"A seagull ate you – that's it. A bird swooped down and made a quick lunch of you!" His voice was another octave higher.

Over in the corner, Jessie hissed at him again.

He watched the cat, a numbness filling his body.

She arched her back, all fur standing on end.

Not numbness; a shadow, a darkness. Yes, as though his body was cloaked in a ghostly, grey fog.

He yelped and jumped to his feet, sending shockwaves of pain through his torso from his stitches.

As quickly as it had appeared, the fog disappeared. For a moment, he imagined the Scottish soldier's face, jeering at him through the window from the garden and then it was gone.

CHAPTER FIFTEEN

It was a hot day, unseasonably warm for Northern Ireland, and Matthew was going to make the most of it. He was only too aware that it was his last day of sick leave. If he took one day more, one single day further, he wouldn't receive any money at all. Not even a token amount of statutory sick pay. It was a tube's life for sure; you worked for the man till you dropped dead.

His own brush with death wasn't far enough behind him. Major surgery, even in a wealthy country like the U.K. still had a risk factor. How close had he been to death? Hard to say? He had lost 300 millilitres of blood. What was that anyway, like a can of fizzy drink?

Getting a grapefruit-sized mass cut out could have led to sepsis, or gangrene, or–

Enough with the neurotic thoughts: what good did they do? He shuddered, in spite of the heat.

As he walked along the street, swinging his Tesco carrier bag with a six pack of Stella, a large bag of O'Donnell's crisps and some pork scratchings, the feeling of eyes on his back made him incline his head a notch towards the left. He glanced in a passing car wing mirror but saw nobody walking behind him. Mad. He was sure of the feeling; the sensation that someone was right behind him. It was an electrical impulse, as though a person was standing too close behind, sending goosebumps along his back and raising all the hairs on his neck.

Maybe just the wind.

Yeah, just the wind. It couldn't be his dead brother, savagely ripped from the husk that had protected it for thirty-three years; the warm, nourishing comfort of a human host in which it could feed and thrive and–

Again with the neurotic thoughts. He gritted his teeth, annoyed at himself. It shouldn't be that hard to have even a touch of mental discipline, yet it seemed impossible for him to control himself.

Thank goodness Sonya was at work. Jessie was better company at the moment. Whenever Sonya appeared at home, on one of the rare nights she didn't arrive home late from work with a paltry excuse, she skulked around the place in a foul mood. At least Jessie was good craic. Seeming determined to cheer him up, the cat had dragged in a live elephant hawk moth that had taken flight in the living room, and a giant harvest spider that she had batted back and forth between paws until he had intervened and freed it in the garden.

The cat provided free entertainment, while his girlfriend provided only scowls.

Invisible eyes bored into his back. He was sure this time; he spun around in a complete one-eighty and looked down the street.

Nothing.

"Brother, if that's you, if you're a ghost haunting me, then could you please do me a favour and fuck off to the afterlife, or hell – or wherever suits you so long as it isn't here? I really could do with the break."

That ought to do it. He spun on the rubber sole of his Adidas trainers and started on down the sunny Oldpark Road towards his house.

As he approached his front garden, Matthew halted to fumble in his pocket for the house key. Reflected in the glass of a nearby bus shelter, a tall, male figure in silhouette lingered behind him. The dark outline looked thickset; not fat, but that of a well-proportioned man with decent muscle mass and broad shoulders.

He gasped and spun once more.

"Are you okay there? Are you lost?"

An old lady appeared from behind, blinking at him through large bifocals. A tiny woman, not a tall athletic man.

He wiped his clammy hairline on his forearm. "No. I, uh, I'm alright."

He hurried towards his garden, slamming the gate behind himself. Once in the house, he leaned his sweaty back against the laminate of the front door and breathed long and slow to steady his heart rate.

What the fuck was going on?

Either he was going crazy, or there were greater forces at work, controlling his life.

Greater forces. Did the silhouette of the tall, athletic man resemble the Scottish soldier in any way? Yes. Then again, so did lots of men that he saw every day, on any given street.

He ran sweaty fingers through his slick hair. Get a grip. Have a beer, chill-out and breathe.

What could he do to relax? He took the pack of Stella through to the back garden and snapped open the ring pull on a can. Leaning back on a recliner, he supped the froth. Ah, that was the life. More drinking in his garden, less visions of the past. Jessie padded across the patio towards him. He opened the bag of pork scratchings and tossed one onto the grass for her.

Matthew's eyes travelled from Jessie eating the pork scratching with jerking, chomping bites, to a reflection in the lower pane of the patio doorway: a fleshy ball on the grass not five feet behind him.

"What the fuck?"

He jumped to his feet. The can of lager overturned spraying froth and yellow liquid across the lawn. The recliner lay on its side. He held his hand against his chest and faced the object he had seen reflected: a basketball thrown over the garden fence from Tommy the knobhead teenager next door.

"My head is *turned*. Maybe I need some effing temazepam to chill the fuck out." Chiding himself aloud seemed to offer consolation, as though the voice of reason came from elsewhere and not himself. Too much isolation wasn't good for him. Not at all.

Sonya wouldn't be home for another four hours at least, and there was no guarantee she'd be in a good mood when she did. Only one thing for it; he would have to go over to Mum and Dad's. Not only would they give him the comfort that he so badly craved at that moment, but they could hopefully answer a few questions about his recently deceased unborn brother too.

CHAPTER SIXTEEN

"It is all in order. It is already happening. He was born on Pluto's return, in the year 1279. The next Pluto's return won't be for another 248 years when Pluto returns to origin. I have calculated the cycle after that, which brings us to the year 1527, and after another 248 years up to 1775. The year after that takes the date into the third millennium in the year of 2023."

The witch sat naked, cross-legged, on a mattress weaved from posies of white flowers: cow's parsley, the Devil's hemlock. Her body was smeared with the blood of a snake, brought from Scotland, as there were none in Ireland. A snake that had emerged from its hole, signifying the beginning of spring, and a new era; caught, carried over waves, and flayed. The dried blood was dark brown, thick linear horizontal stripes, giving her the appearance of a zebra. The upper half of her face from nose to hairline was covered in blood too, giving her green eyes a wild appearance. The lower half of her face had been adorned white with chalk.

"You are sure, my daughter?"

She nodded. "I am certain."

The figure who the witch spoke to wasn't a man, but an imprint of a man. A ghost. It appeared as dark smoke rising from a small fire that the witch had set among kindling in a hollow. Male features could be discerned only after studying the form for a minute or more: a large, broad nose, a beard that hung to the nape of the neck, deep-set, determined eyes. There was a family resemblance between the witch and the ghost.

"Failenn, I need you to do one more thing."

The witch leaned forward, her face eager. "Yes, father, what is it?"

"I need you to take sixteen wheatsheaves. Place them inside the urn you made for the Scotsman. It will ensure the resurrection of the power in our lineage in that time of greater universal energy; the year of 20 and 23. Revenge against those who wronged me, and us, will rain upon them for their misplaced insurrection and betrayal of us, their own townsfolk."

Failenn inhaled through her nose, her chest expanding, and out through her mouth. "It will be done. In the time of Pluto's return, in the year of 20 and 23, when the moon is in conjunction with Saturn, balance will be restored. Those who are honest, those who seek justice, and are willing to work hard will reap the benefits of the fate they now sow."

The fire flickered brighter and as the ghost of Failenn's father faded, a new scene appeared in the midst of the black smoke rising.

A gathering of townsfolk sat on wooden benches inside a long, rectangular building with plain, whitewashed inner walls: the meeting house of Carraig Fhearghais town, near the church, on Church Lane, closer to the walls of the town than the castle.

"I say this is the time for us to be decisive. We need to take fate into our own hands," said one world-weary old man. "The crop failures are rife across Ireland. We are in the grip of famine and yet, three galleys a summer of our wheat supplies are being shipped to Carlisle. It can't go on. Are we to sit back and let our families starve?"

"Yes, they take our supplies for their own greedy garrisons at Dumfries, Ayr and Cockermath while we watch our children go hungry. It can't go on," shouted a woman, red in her face.

"Well, whose fault is that, then?" Another woman, haggard and with dark circles under her eyes from malnourishment, pointed a shaking finger across the room towards a man. He was heavy set with greying hair under a brown suede cap and bushy grey facial hair. "It's Beollan's fault, he's the Keeper of grain."

"I concur. Beollan is at fault!" said another woman, with a small child on her knee.

"Aye, Beollan is to blame," spoke one more man, his teenage son beside him looking thin and pale.

Beollan, the witch's father, showed shock and betrayal all over his face. "I am only doing my duty. My feudal duty is to take orders from King Edward II and send our grain to Carlisle. Who am I to question those orders? I have a wife and daughter of my own to feed. I need the silver."

"Ha, what about silver for us? You don't take orders from Donal O'Neill, or the Red Earl of Ulster, or even from our own Henry Thrapston, Keeper of Carraig Fhearghais Castle. There's talk of a Celtic Alliance with Scotland coming, and yet you are a serf for England. A traitor to your own kin!" shouted a wizened, elderly man.

Next to Beollan, his mousey haired wife and daughter sat wide-eyed and silent. Failenn the witch watched herself in the smoke haze of the fire, her image reflected back as an innocent six year old. The family of three were alone among the townsfolk for being well nourished and well dressed; famine had not touched them.

"Ho, ho, silver for you while the rest of us struggle for even one measly groat to last us a month – and dirt to eat," shouted a woman, with a babe at her breast.

"You are responsible for providing grain to us, your townsfolk, more than those greedy English, robbing us of our food to send Irish provisions and supply defence of their western march. Where's your loyalty, man?"

"I say he's a traitor," shouted one of the men.

"I say we rid ourselves of him – and redistribute the grain. We need to rise up. We can't let England, or its pawns, treat us this way."

Beollan jumped from his seat. He grabbed young Failenn up into his arms and dashed for the door, dragging his wife by her hand. A flurry of men and women followed, but in their haste to grab him, they blocked themselves by their own scrum towards the door. Beollan, hurried outside where his horse and cart waited. With his wife and daughter in the cart, he whipped his horse and they sped off along Church Lane, past his flour mill with its grey stones and thatched roof, and away into the twilight.

As the smoke danced and the fire flickered the witch, Failenn, watched a new scene unfold: the family of three now travelling higher among woodland high up on a hill. Beann Mhadagáin's Peak, overlooking the town of Béal Feirste. Béal Feirste was smaller than Carraig Fhearghais, nothing more than a few wooden huts around a motte and castle, which paled in comparison to Carraig Fhearghais Castle. A simple stone building of two floors surrounded by a wooden bailey atop a small sloping hill, with a brush and reed path leading upwards to the 'castle'. *Béal*, meaning 'river-mouth' and *Feirste* meaning 'sandbar', this village of the 'River-mouth of the sandbar' provided no safe haven for Beollan and his young family.

Word would soon reach the Carraig Fhearghais townsfolk of Beollan's whereabouts in Béal Feirste, the obvious place where a Keeper of Grain would flee to. No, it was certain death to go there. Hiding in the woodland of Beann Mhadagáin's Peak was the safest choice until Beollan thought of what course of action to take.

But his plan was foiled before it had even been fully conceived.

"There he is! There is the traitor. Grab him!"

Men carrying flaming torches. Women following with vicious dogs on tethers, snarling and baring their teeth. They all wanted blood: Beollan's blood.

The family of three dashed out of the woodland and scrambled on upwards to higher ground where a thick, dark expanse of heather bushes might swallow them up and give cover until morning.

But the hands and feet behind them were too fast, fuelled by rage, and hunger, and desperation.

"Beollan, meaning glowing fire. An appropriate name, for tonight, he of the glowing fire on Beann Mhadagáin's Peak will burn bright all the way from Béal Feirste, across the Lough, to Carraig Fhearghais, beyond it to Latharna, and out over the North channel. His ashes will reach the English Lords as a message that we will fight back, and they will never take away what is ours."

Young Failenn, only six years old, tore free of the hands that held her and stood her ground facing the man who had spoken. "You do that and you will feel my wrath. You – not the English – will feel the fury of my revenge. You wait and see. For as long as it takes, I will pay back all of you."

CHAPTER SEVENTEEN

"Hello? Are you just going to sit there and ignore me?"

Matthew blinked to wet his dry eyes and registered Sonya bending down in front of him, waving her hand.

"Earth to Matty, are you there? Hello?"

He was in his back garden with his can of Stella, pork scratchings and Jessie near his feet, stretched out in the last remaining sun before it set. She stood over his recliner, her denim dungarees covered in soil from her dig, and clicked her fingers a few inches from his face.

He brushed her hand away. "Lay off, I can hear you. I just zoned out."

She scoffed. "Zoned out? I was calling for like, a million years and you just sat there blanking me. Did you have another one of your freak-outs?"

Why did she have to be as annoying as possible? "If you are referring to my visions when you say freak-outs, then yes, I saw another scene from the past. Only this one was different. It was like a scene within a scene."

She flopped down on the grass and started playing with Jessie's tail, which flicked from side to side in the sunlight. "Go on then, I'm all ears."

He had half a mind to tell her that she shouldn't flatter herself as he didn't need her listening, but there was no point goading her; and if truth be told, he did want to get it off his chest. "I saw the witch again. Her name was Failenn. It's an old Irish name meaning seagull. Anyway, she was talking to the ghost of her father who had appeared in the middle of a bonfire."

"As you do," she said, with a smirk.

He rolled his eyes. "Do you want to hear this, or not?"

"Go on then." A bored expression settled on her face.

"He was asking her to take revenge against sixteen people who had wronged him – sixteen people who had burned him alive on Beann Mhadagáin's Peak. You know, Cavehill today?"

Now was her turn to roll her eyes. "I know what Cavehill used to be called. Ben Madigan, or the Irish, Beann Mhadagáin, if you like. I'm an archaeologist, for fuck's sake."

He ignored her. "They burned him in front of her, when she was only a girl."

"Did you get to see the good part at least – him burning up in flames?"

He tossed his head in disbelief. "This wasn't like watching a film. This really happened in medieval times in this country. Why would I find a man burning to death entertaining? I could smell his skin cooking, are you mad?"

"Alright, keep your hair on. So, what happened? Did she go and get a crossbow and, like, shoot all sixteen of them right in the head?"

Jessie awoke at that moment, raised her front left paw, and scrabbed Sonya. Blood seeped from a deep, four-inch scratch on the back of her hand.

"Ow, Jessie, what's got into you?" She cradled her injured hand.

"See? It's a sign. Just like us going up on Cavehill a few days before my surgery. That was a sign too," he said. "We were right near the spot where Beollan was torched by an angry mob."

She sucked the gash on her hand. "What did they burn him for anyway?"

"He was the Keeper of Grain in Carrickfergus. His job was to supply wheat for export to the English garrisons in Carlisle. The townspeople were upset as they were starving because of war, and famine, while he and his family were rich."

She made fish lips at him. "Listen, even if all this was real, it still happened, like, seven hundred years ago. What does it matter to our lives today?"

He guffawed. "Imagine that coming from an archaeologist!"

Her cheeks turned crimson. "You know what I'm saying. Failenn and her dad Beollan, and all sixteen of the murderers who burned him alive, are all dead. What relevance does it have to anyone living today?"

"Aye, but see that's the thing, it *is* relevant to today. Failenn said all this creepy stuff, numerology you know, and something about Pluto's return. Apparently, a Pluto's return in cosmology happens every 248 years. She said that someone – a man – was born in the year 1279A.D. If you keep adding 248 onto that date, it brings it into the present. It brings it to this year – 2023."

"Pluto." She looked thoughtful. "That's the god of the Underworld in Greek mythology. But who was the man?"

He shrugged. "An antichrist figure, maybe, if they were religious people?"

Jessie circled Sonya, rubbing herself all over her owner, then settled in her lap. Her hand fell to stroking the cat in long, sweeping, idle moves. "You're so funny, Matty. Look at you getting all worked-up about a dream you had."

"For the last time, it wasn't a dream. It was a vision. And I'm not worked up, but you know what? It wouldn't be the most irrational thing in the world to get upset about dreams of witchcraft and occult numerology, would it?"

She grinned. "All that aside, I'm glad it's your last day of sick leave. I really think getting stuck back into work is the best thing for you. You've had too much time off brooding about your surgery."

Brooding. She made it seem like he was a fat hen sitting on an egg. "You sound exactly like that hospital appointed shrink I've been forced to see."

"Don't knock the help, it's the best thing that's happened to you recently. All I'm saying is that you need to take charge of your life. You've been wallowing too much, preoccupied with weird shit, and all."

He sucked in air. "Wallowing? Preoccupied with what? Deciphering visions from the past? Shouldn't that be your job? You should be helping me make sense of these clues I've been getting from the past."

She shrieked with laughter, then clapped a hand over her mouth. "Sorry babe, but you crack me up. That's just too *cute*. You really think these strange notions you've been getting actually mean something in reality? Trust me Matty, archaeology is my profession and you need *evidence* to say that something has a connection to the past. Having funny daydreams – or nightmares – isn't cause to go off on a treasure hunt trying to work out if there's any basis in reality. Heck, if my dreams were to have any basis in reality then I'd be married to Viggo Mortensen dressed up like Aragorn. Whew!"

Matthew couldn't believe what he had just heard. Sonya fanned herself with her hand; he didn't give a shit if she was thinking of an actor in fantasy movie garb instead of him. She was calling him irrational. Worse: histrionic.

"You don't believe me at all, do you? About any of it. The witch. The clay urn. The Scottish soldier. Even when I have evidence – the clay urn that you gave me yourself!"

"That's just a pot." She flapped her hand dismissively. "Listen, I believe you've had funny dreams lately, but I think that's all they are – dreams. And I think that to read into them any more than what you've been doing is–"

"Is what? Crazy?" He glared at her.

104

She sighed. "It just isn't very masculine, that's all. It's sort of *sissy-ish*, in fact."

He huffed. "What's that supposed to mean? Are you calling me a wuss?"

She ran her hand backwards through Jessie's fur, making the cat hiss and bristle. "All I'm saying is that you need to man-up a bit and take charge of your life."

"Man-up? Take charge?" He intoned each word as if she'd issued a string of profanities at him.

"Yes," she said, her voice flat. "Why don't you just grow a pair, Matthew?"

"That's rich!" He stood up quick as a flash, sending his recliner keeling over sideways. "Imagine telling a man who just had part of himself cut away to 'grow a pair'? Such a big woman, kicking a man when he's down! As if life doesn't give me enough shit and now my own girlfriend thinks I'm cuckoo."

She dropped her jaw, her face blotchy with surprise. Both hands were up in protest, but he didn't wait for her to say anything. He stomped across the garden and through the house. Going over to his parent's house for some respite was the best plan he had in mind for the time being; anything to get away from her before he said something he regretted.

CHAPTER EIGHTEEN

Matthew stared at the mug of tea in his cupped hands and ran his thumbs around the rim. The smiley face on the front goaded him, as though saying *I'm happy and you're not. What would you give to be me, you bastard?* He swallowed sour saliva in his mouth and turned the mug around so his nemesis couldn't taunt him anymore.

"I'm sure she'll come round, love. It's just a bad patch."

He looked up at his mum. Pity, not hope, showed in her expression. He buried his face in his mug and slurped his tea.

"It's a bad patch that I don't know how to fix. I've tried time and again to get a conversation going between us, but then all she wants to do is make a sarky comment and it sets me off. It's like, all she wants to do is provoke me – this was even before the surgery."

His dad, who had been tight-lipped and awkward during all the relationship chat, perked up at the change in topic. "How's your stitches doing anyway, son? Are they still giving you pain?"

He pulled his polo shirt up and showed the scar. "They itch more than they hurt, though I suppose that's a good thing, isn't it? It must mean they're healing."

His mum pointed at his abdomen. "It's scary to think that – something like that – was inside of you all these years."

Something like that. She said it with a gulp of disgust. It hadn't occurred to him to think of how knowledge of the foetus-in-foetu must have affected her. It was his unborn brother, a life he had no control over having created, but it was her child – a son she had conceived. On top of that, it had been neither a live birth or a still birth. It had been a living deformity, a ball of human tissue and organic structures, not alive, but not dead.

It made him shiver. "Actually, about that, mum. Did you know that you had been expecting twins? Or did you think it was going to be just me?"

"I never for a moment thought that there was another foetus in there, I was only ever expecting you. But there was one time when I had a very odd feeling, that I won't ever forget," she said, a wistful look on her face.

"What happened?" He leaned forward, hunching over his cupped mug.

"I must have only been a few weeks into pregnancy at that time, and I was in the kitchen doing the dishes. There was a very strange sky, so unusual that I stopped what I was doing and went to the back door to look out. The sunset looked like an egg-yolk that had smeared all over the sky, like when you crack an egg in the pan and it breaks its membrane and goes everywhere. There were streaks of red running through it too, red as blood. I suffered a searing pain at that moment, which made me cry out. I managed to get myself to the bathroom, hobbling of course, and blood was dripping down my legs. I thought I was losing you – I thought the sunset was prophetic. But when I went for an emergency check, you were fine. Your heartbeat was strong – we could see the tiny pumping motion on the screen when they did an ultrasound. Now looking back, that must have been the death of your brother – not you."

He shook his head. "Not death. He didn't die. He was absorbed into my body."

"It must have been the moment when the two of you merged then," she said with a sniff.

"Could've been worse," said his dad. "At least you didn't end up as Siamese twins. Life chances for both of you would've been much worse if that were the case. You both might've died. At least they were able to remove the other one from you and now you can go on living a normal life."

The other one. He noted how his dad gave a deflective wave of the hand as he said the words. Guess the notion of an unborn parasitic twin child was hard for his dad to process too. "Doesn't matter whether I was a Siamese twin or had a foetus-in-foetu – Sonya probably thinks I'm a freak no matter what."

"Oh silly, don't say that. She loves you. I'm sure she doesn't think any such thing at all," said his mum.

He would've believed her, had she not lowered her eyes and looked elsewhere while saying the last three words.

"Youse two don't think I'm a freak – do you?" He raised his head from his mug and held his mum's gaze, not to miss a thing. The fact that she looked green didn't reassure him.

His mum dismissed his question with a wave. "Let's get our minds off such morbid topics. You're young and you're fit and you have a steady job. If Sonya thinks you're anything other than perfect, then more fool her."

So, they *did* think he was a freak; at least, his mum did. Matthew's nostrils flared as he breathed in a noisy lungful of air, hoping the oxygen would help to calm him. Was nobody on his side? Not Sonya, not his mum—

"Ach, Sylvia, you're making things worse for him. Of course he feels like a freak – he's entitled to – what are the odds of a parasitic twin? One in half a million? He's certainly unique, I'll give him that," said his dad.

"Thanks dad." His voice sounded much more weary than intended. He appreciated his dad's honesty; better than his mum glossing over the truth to spare his feelings, or Sonya being outright hostile.

"What about the strange dreams you'd been having? Did they stop after the surgery?" His mum still had a guilty look on her face. He knew she was changing the topic again to deflect as she felt uncomfortable.

"No. In fact, they've intensified," he said.

She raised her eyebrows. "Oh dear. I had half-hoped it was similar to getting nightmares after eating rich food."

"My parasitic brother wasn't rich food, mum," he said.

She flat-out blushed at that retort. Without saying anything further, she lifted the three empty tea mugs and bustled into the kitchen.

"Don't mind her, it's been hard on her too. She's been worried about you – after the surgery."

He studied his dad's face. What was with the slight pause before he said, *after the surgery*? Did that mean she was worried about his mental health, but his dad tried to cover his tracks by throwing that in at the last minute? Or was he being too paranoid?

"Yeah, her and everyone else. All my colleagues think I'm touched in the head after I saw a woman – the witch from my dreams – in one of the holding pens at work. Sonya thinks I'm reading too much into the dreams too. She straight up laughed in my face and told me I was taking it all too seriously. But I've got the urn at home as proof. Sonya gave it to me herself, she got it from her dig in Carrick and gave it to me to cheer me up after my surgery."

His dad's brow creased. "The clay urn from your dream? The one you said was made with the Scottish soldier's blood?"

Impressive. Not only had his dad actually been listening to him but had remembered what he'd said, and he had told him that dream on the phone weeks ago. "Aye, that's right. The witch – her name was Failenn – made it as an amulet for him so that the Scots would be successful in their Irish campaign."

His dad went on. "That was very thoughtful of Sonya to give it to you as a present. She must have made it for you to look like the one in your dream. Don't you think that was a great idea, as a boost, while you were convalescing after your surgery?"

His hopes, which had momentarily been raised, were dashed on the floor like a metaphorical occult urn splintering into thousands of shards. He stood up. "I'd better be on my way. I have a lot on my mind at the moment. I need to rest this weekend, as I'm starting back to work on Monday, and I have to get in the right head space."

"Son wait, I hope you didn't take that the wrong way—"

He paused and looked down over the bridge of his nose at his dad, then his mum in turn. "I'll see youse around."

CHAPTER NINETEEN

Was anyone on his side? Sonya thought he was touched in the head. His mum and dad thought he was touched in the head. Nobody took his visions seriously. They were more than mere dreams; they were a foretelling of doom from the past and a prophecy of past evil that had come to exact revenge in the present.

With a sigh, he entered his house and wiped his feet on the door mat. The smell of Sonya's perfume lingered in the hallway. She didn't wear perfume often, only for special occasions. Did that mean she had left recently? But, where to?

He went through all the rooms of the house in turn. Yep, definitely gone. His gaze fell to a note on his bedside table.

Matthew, I've gone away for a few days. Maybe I'm staying with a fantasy man. Yeah, maybe I've found my Aragorn. Ha, ha, ha. Your Sugar.

Hmph. What a strange note. Had Sonya ever left him a note, in the twelve years they'd been together? Maybe once when she'd misplaced her phone and wanted him to pick up more milk.

He checked the wardrobe. It had been emptied by half. He pulled open the drawers that she used. All were empty. Who went away for a few days and took the majority of their clothes with them?

With a sinking feeling in his gut, he trudged downstairs. There was no sign of Jessie anywhere. The housecat rarely escaped, to the point where Sonya made a song and dance if she did. He flipped the cupboard under the kitchen sink open, the one where Sonya stored Jessie's food.

Empty.

He kicked it shut, swung the fridge open and grabbed the last can of Stella. Sonya had left him. Life was just *great*. Just effing great.

The can sprayed beer all over the living room, splattering foam on the rug. Sonya wasn't there to moan; he stomped on it a few times until it had all absorbed. No point being clean now, what was the point? Besides, it was *her* rug anyway.

The urn on the fireplace drew his eye. She hadn't taken it with her. He strode across the room where it sat on the mantelpiece level with his heart. He had half a mind to smash it, but instead, put his can of Stella in it. The bottom of the can slotted in as though the urn had been made for it.

Was that desecration of a sacrilegious artefact? He didn't know what possessed him to do it. It was an object associated with black magic; but he was already cursed anyway, so desecrating it couldn't possibly cause him any further harm.

With his cupped hands around the urn, he drank his beer. Condensation from the can seeped into the clay, but he didn't care. Let Failenn come for him. She was going to come for him anyway, so might as well speed up her move. Why she was coming after him though, was anyone's guess. What had he to do with the soldiers at Carrickfergus, both Anglo-Irish and Scottish?

He recalled the vision of Henry Thrapston speaking inside Carrickfergus Castle, and how he had seen this directly through the eyes of Aymer, one of the soldiers. What if he, Matthew, was a descendant of Aymer; a great-great-times-twenty-grandson, or something?

Or worse; a cold flow in his bloodstream chilled his body. What if he was a reincarnation of Aymer?

Nonsense. Matthew shook his head. Ghosts – and reincarnation – didn't exist. He was an atheist. Death was the end of life. The human body, like that of any other animal, became worm food after death.

The agnostic in him elbowed the atheist aside, with a small voice of protest: where was the proof that death was the end of everything? What if the *mind* could live on again, in another life, even if the body died?

What if he had actually *been* an Anglo-Irish soldier in the year 1315 at Carrickfergus? What if Aymer had harmed Failenn in some way? If so, it would explain why he had suddenly started having strange dreams.

He shivered at the wave of psychic meltwater pouring an icy river over him. Every sense in his body told him he was right.

With the urn up at eye level, close to the bridge of his nose, he could see every tiny stone and quartz piece embedded in the clay. "Failenn, if I did something to wrong you in a past life, then I'm sorry. But, please don't take your revenge on me. I'm Matthew. I'm a portal inspector at Larne, not Aymer, a soldier at Carrickfergus. I'm a good person, not a killer. If there's something I can do to fix a past mistake, then let me do it now. Give me a chance to right that wrong. Just don't unleash your wrath on me. I'm only one man, not an Anglo-Irish army."

What about the other fifteen people from the past? If his hunch was right, that he was a reincarnated soldier from Carrickfergus, fighting against the Scottish conquest of Edward the Bruce in Ireland, then Failenn would come after fifteen other reincarnated souls too; wherever they were in the world.

Sixteen townsfolk in Carrickfergus had chased Failenn's father, Beollan, to Cavehill and had burned him alive. He could understand how she must have felt, especially since she had only been a girl when she had witnessed the murder of her father. It would've been a horrific sight for an adult, but even more traumatising for a child. He tried to harness his feeling of compassion for her and held the urn against his chest, imagining healing waves radiating out of his heart and into the urn.

His thoughts jumped back to Sonya. She had found the urn at her dig in Carrickfergus. Maybe the site where she had found it, in situ, was the location of Failenn's cottage from his past visions. When he was back to work on Monday he would stop by his girlfriend's dig in Carrickfergus, on the way home from his shift in Larne, and see the exact site of where the witch had once lived. There, he was sure he could make a stronger healing connection; hopefully enough to stop whatever vengeful plans her ghost had in store.

CHAPTER TWENTY

The seagulls swooped low over the sea, diving down close to the choppy waves, then veered upwards into the stormy grey skies. The others kept intercutting, weaving in front of him from left to right. He wasn't concerned with their movements; like him they were sentient beings. What he was concerned with was how he had Matthew's consciousness. Metaphysically, there was no difference from Matthew, portal inspector at Larne, and unnamed seagull of the North Channel.

How did he know it was the North Channel, a strip of water separating Northern Ireland and Scotland, that he flew over? He didn't. Matthew-seagull swooped closer to land; he could use the coastline to get an idea of where he was. The distinctive basalt cliffs were familiar, the black rocks not dissimilar from the modern day, in 2023. He knew where he was; the only difference was the missing white, latticed suspension bridge over the deep inlets and gullies. This was the Gobbins Cliff Path, near Islandmagee, close to Larne.

Matthew-seagull swooped back upwards now that he had his bearings. Travelling further south along the coastline from Islandmagee led to Whitehead, where in 2023, Blackhead Lighthouse would have stood on the edge of Belfast Lough. But not then, back in 1315, when an unnamed seagull became the eyes and ears for Matthew of a distant, medieval past. It was a psionic ability that could be attributed to only one person, who lately he had become intimately connected with: Failenn, the witch from Carrickfergus, who had come to haunt him for reasons that he still did not fully understand. Failenn, who had transferred her mind into the body of a seagull, Failenn who had created a portal with Matthew in the present, through which he could see the past from high above the land.

Far below, on the black-grey storm waves, thirteen galleys carrying thirty crannocks of wheat were buffeted and smashed by powerful waves. The galleys, with their low freeboards sitting well below the water line, were vulnerable to the rough, grey water with its large swells. Twenty-five oars on each side propelled them forward, and a red flag bearing three gold lions, representing England, Normandy and Aquitaine under the House of Plantagenet, rippled above a large, single white sail. The galleys rose on the swells of grey-tipped stormy crests and sank into dangerous black troughs. They were sailed by Edward II's victuallers upon order from the crown and carried grain to supply the defenders at Carrickfergus against the Scottish garrisons surrounding the castle. Once in the safety of the Belfast Lough, they would be protected by the hills on both sides: modern day Bangor on the left and Whitehead on the right, sheltering them from the worst ravages of the sea. But they weren't there yet. All thirteen were scattered by the storm raging in the North Channel. Three galleys changed course towards Whitehaven, across the sea in England, while another four made it to Skinburness, further north along the coast from Whitehaven. The rest perished, smashed against the looming, black basalt cliffs stretching northwards from Whitehead to Larne in Northern Ireland, only known then as Ulster.

Matthew-seagull swooped downwards once more until soon it flew towards the rocky promontory on which sat Carrickfergus Castle. At the postern gate, men waited to receive the much-needed grain from the thirteen galleys, that would never come. Crossbowmen stood ready at the machicolations over the portcullis at the front, while archers lined the walls of the inner ward. They waited for an attack that wouldn't come. Where were the Scotsmen with ladders waiting to climb the walls? Where were the catapults? What about the battering rams? The Scottish garrison had occupied the town since they had sacked it in May 1315. What were they waiting for?

When the seagull glided low over the charred town, Matthew floated light as a discarded tail feather on a soft breeze, watching the bird soar away. His consciousness drifted lower, through the thatched roof of a shabby house. It was the only house that hadn't been torched, the sole dwelling on the street where the inhabitants hadn't been driven out or killed by the Scottish garrison. Six Scottish soldiers wearing the yellow tunics emblazoned with the red lions of Edward Bruce occupied most of the space in the tiny hovel. One woman stood with her back to the room as she filled earthenware cups with broth from a steaming pot on the hearth. When she turned to pass the broth around, he recognised the witch, Failenn.

The first soldier sniffed the broth with a suspicious glare. "Where did you get supplies to make a broth when the rest of the country is in famine and shortage?"

Failenn smiled. "I gather the herbs I need from Beann Mhadagáin's Peak. They grow well on a spot that is sacred to me."

The same soldier's upper lip crumpled in distaste. "It's not poison, is it?"

"Drink it. She's not one of them." It was the soldier whose blood Failenn had used to make an occult urn for necromantic purposes; that of ensuring a Scottish victory over the Anglo-Irish.

"Just because you are bedding the woman doesn't make her trustworthy – or an ally. You speak with your loins, Colbyn."

Five soldiers laughed. One glowered. Colbyn was not happy with his fellow foot-soldiers. "The plan will work, if you do what we say. Drink the broth. It is more than mere subsistence. There is nutrition in it to nurture your soul as well as your body. We have a long time to wait. Those inside Carraig Fhearghais Castle have no way to escape. All we have to do is keep our strength, bide our time, and starve them out."

The witch grinned as she watched the soldiers drink. "Success is guaranteed. Revenge will be mine."

CHAPTER TWENTY-ONE

Sonya, I got your note. Can you text me back?

No response. Unusual for her, who usually texted back straightaway; though not lately. Lately she had taken to ignoring his texts for several hours, or even a whole day, before replying. He was being ghosted for sure, the distance between them stretching ever further.

I need to see you. I'm on my way to your work.

Matthew sent the text with one hand while he cruised along the M2 from Larne towards Carrickfergus. Lucky for him that his first shift back after his sick leave had ended at 4PM, the reduced hours to give him a phased return; he would have time to swing by her excavation and catch her before they wrapped up the dig for the evening at 5 o'clock.

He was sure that she was receiving his texts. Sonya said she always kept her phone with her in the trench; all the archaeologists were encouraged to keep them handy in case of emergency, especially on larger sites. It didn't matter if she wasn't going to respond, he would see her soon at any rate, and hopefully break the impasse between them.

As he rounded a corner into the archaeological site, a small brown-haired woman stepped into the middle of the bumpy road. He veered right to avoid her, and the car lurched into a gulley. Bushy branches from the overgrown hedgerow crunched against the windscreen. No sign of her in the rear-view mirror. It had to be Failenn. Was it a ghost? She looked exactly as he had seen her crouching in the cattle pen at work, exactly the same as in his medieval visions. Yes, she had to be a ghost, or an entity, of some description. He had always imagined ghosts to be wispy and vapourish, but Failenn was so real. So solid.

He slammed his foot on the gas in an effort to get the front and rear wheels on the right side unstuck, and stones crunched against the engine casing as the car lurched out of the gulley. A groan at the sound of inevitable damage to his car; he was nowhere near due an upgrade on his current loan being only one year into a three-year plan. He definitely didn't have the cash handy to get it repaired. Failenn didn't want him coming near the location of her historical abode; and probably didn't want him getting near Sonya either.

The car rattled as it trundled the short, remaining road into a small carpark. When he got out, he assessed the damage: the bumper was hanging off on the right side, which had been making the rattling noise as it dragged over the stones. He sighed before looking around, expecting Failenn's ghostly form to materialise behind him. Wonder what other tricks she had up her sleeve for him?

"I told you, Failenn, I'm not an enemy. Whatever my spirit did in a past life isn't me as I am today. I have no grief with you, so please don't give me any in return. I'm here to see my girlfriend. I'd appreciate it if you didn't stand in the way of that."

A thud against the top of his head made him throw both hands over his head and crouch. A seagull flew away. It circled around and dived down at him, and a heavy wing smacked his face. The bird swooping down again was no coincidence; it was an orchestrated attack, straight out of Hitchcock's *The Birds*.

Failenn: seagull. Her name meant seagull in medieval Irish, derived from the proto-Celtic name Welanna. Welanna, which became in old Irish, Failenn. Why did he know this? Because Failenn wanted him to. Why was he connected to Failenn? A hatred of his soul spanning seven centuries.

"Failenn, if Aymer did anything wrong to you, or to your father Beollan, then I'm sorry. I'm sorry if you both got hurt. But Aymer isn't me. It has nothing to do with me, or my life today. Can we not let go of the past and let our spirits be free – yours, mine, your father's, Colbyn's – all the people involved who have a grievance? It was a brutal time, back then in history, but all people did was what they could to survive – and what they believed was right, even if it was wrong."

The seagull swooped down again, smacking him again with its powerful wing. Matthew ducked and shielded his face with both arms.

As the seagull veered around ready to launch another assault, he dashed back to his car. The bird flew towards the windscreen twice, its feet tapping against the glass, though knew better than to attack in a losing battle. It didn't launch a third offensive; the seagull took to the sky and flew out over Belfast Lough.

With a cautious check of the sky in all directions, he slipped out of his car and hurried towards Sonya's dig. He had met Tony, her supervisor on one occasion at the pub a few years back and recognised him, even wearing a yellow hard hat and high visibility vest.

"Alright there Tony. I'm just looking for Sonya. Is she about?" His eyes flitted behind Sonya's boss to the small team of seven archaeologists, busy surveying, digging or drawing. No sign of his girlfriend anywhere.

Tony gawped at him. "Matthew! Good to see you, mate. I thought she was with you? She said you were sick and that she had to go home to look after you. She left about an hour ago."

He fumed. So, Sonya was using his name in her lies to her boss? "I'd had surgery, but I'm all recovered now, this was my first day back at work. You've no idea where else she might have gone then, do you?"

Tony shook his head. He turned to the team of archaeologists and shouted. "Chris, could you c'mere a moment?"

The seven archaeologists were working in pairs; all except for the one man who stood up from his trench where he had been trowelling a dark splodge of earth. Must have been Sonya's teammate.

"What's the craic?" said Chris, his eyes on Matthew.

"This is Sonya's partner. He's looking for her. She didn't say anything to you before she left, did she?" said Tony.

Chris looked at Tony with a puzzled face. "Not to me, but she was on the phone to someone before she left. Said she'd meet whoever it was in Robinsons." He turned to Matthew. "I assumed it was you she was talking to. I could hear a muffled voice on the other end, and it sounded like a gruff voice, you know. A fella's voice."

He swallowed a bitter lump. That was enough proof. Sonya was doing the dirty on him, cheating right under his nose. There was no other explanation for her aloofness and at times, downright hostility. "Listen, thanks for letting me know. Obviously it's not what I was hoping to hear. I was wanting to see her here. But, since I'm here anyway, I was wondering if you'd allow me to have a quick look at the spot where she's been working – what's the terminology you archaeologist's use? The feature?"

Chris nodded. "We've both been excavating a medieval hearth. See that black area over there? Sonya made a lovely find just a few weeks ago – an intricate funerary urn, not in the usual style for the time period either."

"I know." He spoke in a solemn voice. "She gave it to me as a present."

Tony and Chris both blanched.

"She gave it to you?" Tony's voice was an octave higher with rage. "You mean to say, she took home an artefact?"

He nodded slowly, savouring the moment of payback to Sonya for cheating.

Tony inhaled, his chest swelling, exposing the tendons in his neck. "Do you still have it?"

"It's on the mantelpiece over the electric fireplace in my house. I've been using it as a cup holder for my beer."

Tony looked like he was going to be sick. Chris was pale.

"Is there any way you could bring it back to us, preferably as soon as possible?"

A lightbulb switched on in his head. What if Failenn was angry because her sacred urn had been stolen? It wouldn't explain all of the paranormal events that had been happening, but might explain why the witch's rage seemed to have intensified towards him lately.

"I'll drop it off tomorrow on my way to work. Honestly, I'll be glad to get rid of it. There's bad energy around it. That thing was made with blood magic," he said. "Well, since I'm coming back anyway, would you mind if I have a look at the hearth tomorrow? I think I'll be on my way now. I'm going to take a wee detour to Robinsons on my way home."

Tony offered a sympathetic slap on his arm. "Good luck, mate. Don't deck the guy too hard, alright?"

CHAPTER TWENTY-TWO

Matthew hurried along Great Victoria Street towards Robinsons. The historic pub, with its black facade and gold lettering, lay ahead. A group of laughing tourists carrying backpacks crossed the busy street from the Europa Hotel opposite and blocked the footpath in front of him as they walked towards the famous Crown Liquor Saloon. He weaved through the throng into Robinsons. Life seemed intent on stopping him from seeing Sonya; if it wasn't an aggressive seagull swooping down, or the vengeful ghost of a witch, it was a crowd of sightseers blocking his way.

Why? Why did Sonya have to cheat on him?

He needed to get to her and ask her. Yes, they had been distant for a while, and yes, his surgery had added extra stress that they didn't need; but nothing that they couldn't have worked out given time. His forehead tightened and tears threatened to spring from his eyes. He pressed his eyelids shut, forcing them away and strode into Robinsons, between the jovial doormen. How nice for others to be so carefree; if only his own life was so easy.

Would he catch the despicable cheater right in the middle of her dirty rotten affair? Hopefully. It might propel him into a decision about what to do with his relationship. How could she do that to him? Twelve years; he sighed. Twelve fucking years; he gritted his teeth. Another sigh to clear away the anger. He thought back to his last post-operative chat with Sonya when he told her to go and get another man; a better man. Had she really taken him seriously about that? Had she really gone out, while he had been lying in his hospital bed looking like an Egyptian Mummy, and found a better-looking man with a better job?

He spotted her amidst the drinkers after a few minutes scouring the faces in the pub. His girlfriend's flame red hair stood out a mile. She was in a booth towards the left side of the pub, beside the White Star Line Titanic memorabilia in glass cases. She wasn't alone: a man laughed and talked with her. Matthew scoffed to himself; maybe the Titanic was a metaphor for their relationship. Doomed.

Her companion was a classic 'tall, dark and handsome' type. They sat close, shoulder to shoulder, in a booth but didn't hold hands or cuddle. The closeness suggested to him that their relationship was more than platonic: flirting, a hint of something more.

The fact that she had slipped out of work early to see her companion in private, away from the prying eyes of her archaeology colleagues, and certainly away from him showed that she knew her liaison was illicit. He huffed as he made a beeline for her booth.

"Sonya. Didn't expect you to be here. And I see you have company?"

Sonya and her mystery man looked up. While the man studied Matthew with a sullen gaze, disgruntled that he had interrupted their conversation, Sonya immediately skidded away from him on the seat. She looked like a *scundered* teenager who had been caught doing hanky-panky in class; her hands fell into her lap and she fixed doe-eyes on Matthew, looking the picture of innocence. The only giveaway was her cheeks, which had flushed as red as her hair.

Didn't seem like he was going to get any answers, seeing as she was playing coy. "Who's this, then?" He nodded towards her secret lover.

She flicked her hair back off her shoulder and looked along the bridge of her nose at him. "This here – this is – Aragorn."

"Aragorn," the mystery man guffawed. He gave her a playful nudge with his elbow.

Sonya flashed her loverboy a flirtatious smile. Matthew seethed. He hadn't seen smiles like those directed at him since the early days of when they had first started going out. When she saw that he had noticed, she covered her indiscretion with her hand.

Was she for real? His own girlfriend was shamelessly throwing herself at her rugged mystery man, and in doing so, disrespecting both of them. The *audacity*. Rude cow: how dare she make light of the situation. "I'm sure it is. What's his real name then?"

"I'm Ben," said the man, with a confident smile, bold as brass.

He studied Ben, resisting the urge to grab him by the scruff, deck him one on the jaw, and send him smashing through the glass of the Titanic displays. How could the bastard be so blasé when he had nicked another man's girlfriend?

Or, could there be a possibility that Ben didn't know Sonya wasn't single? Matthew turned to him. "Do you know who I am?"

"I think so," said Ben. "You're Andrew, right? Sonya's housemate?"

"I'm Matthew, and I'm her boyfriend, not her housemate," he said, curt and cold. He turned to Sonya, unblinking. "At least, I thought I was."

She jostled in her seat. "Um, Ben and I were just catching up."

"Catching up? How long has this been going on?" He demanded.

She cocked her head to the left, then right; a curious gesture, more like a boxer warming up for a match than a lover having a romantic after-work drink with their other half. "An hour. Maybe two."

Two hours. Sarky bitch. She didn't have even one iota of remorse. In fact, it seemed more like she was *flaunting* her liaison on purpose as though to say: *this is my upgrade fella. He's taller than you, better-looking than you. He's smarter than you too. Nope, you're just second-fiddle now, so you better get used to it as there's not one fucking thing you can do about it.*

He looked again at Ben. His dark, closely cropped hair and beard, and his deep-set brown eyes, were ruggedly handsome; and strikingly familiar. Did he know Ben from somewhere? But where?

It couldn't possibly be the Scottish soldier from the fourteenth century, could it? Thingmajig, what was his name: Colbyn?

He brushed the thought away. What a ridiculous notion. Here sat a flesh and blood man, as real as he was. How old was Ben anyway: late twenties? Early thirties, like he was? If the ghost of Colbyn from medieval Scotland had been born again into a baby in twenty-first century Northern Ireland, and grown up in Belfast, then he would have come looking for him sooner to exact revenge, would he not? If they were as old as each other, both 'nineties kids', then Failenn would have made sure that Colbyn – Ben – had been bullying him since they were children, surely?

There had to be a better explanation. The most logical explanation was that Sonya had got him so riled up, so upset, that he was looking to make patterns and find connections when there weren't any. For, if a supernatural reason explained what was going on, then it would be easier to forgive people – wouldn't it? If the easy explanation was that Sonya was being telepathically coerced by, say Failenn, then that would make her an innocent victim rather than a guilty, complicit cheater?

He looked again at his girlfriend, who looked back with a neutral expression. No guilt, but no love either; as bland and expressionless as two new colleagues, meeting as strangers for the first time.

How depressing. He plopped down on the seat opposite Sonya and her lover, making a heavy thud on the fake leather. No wonder she had found herself a new bit-on-the-side. What did he have to offer her? Nothing much.

"How are you feeling?" She nudged him with her toe, her long leg bridging the gap between them.

He searched her face. "Are you for real? Are you really asking me that?"

She offered a weak smile. "I meant about your stitches."

"Don't try to change the topic," he huffed. "You sit here with some fancy-man while I'm recovering from major surgery at home, and you try to tell me it's an innocent catch up? I wasn't born yesterday, Sonya."

Ben looked from Sonya to Matthew and back again at Sonya. "What's going on?"

"Nothing," she said, irritation etched all over her face.

Matthew shook his head in disbelief. "Answer me this and I'll tell you what's on my mind. Are you having an affair?"

Sonya's eyes widened with shock, though he couldn't help but sense she was faking it. Was there a hint of pity at him in her gaze?

"That is such an insult! You've never asked me such a thing in the whole twelve years we've lived together."

Lived together. Not *been* together, *lived* together. Unbelievable. She was still perpetuating the lie to Ben that they were housemates. "Sonya, stop. Just stop. What are you going to tell me next – that he's your long-lost cousin that you didn't know you had?"

He stood up and dusted his trousers, to brush off Sonya and her lies. Without saying a word, he stomped towards the door. As he cast one last glance back, he saw her feigning innocence and Ben's angry scowl as he glowered at her, his hands upturned with incredulity. Let the despicable cheater sort out her own mess. She could have Ben, if he wanted such a love-rat for a romantic partner. For all he knew, they deserved each other. Though he, for one, deserved better.

CHAPTER TWENTY-THREE

The wind stung Matthew's eyes, making rivulets of tears over his cheeks, as he hurried along Castle Lane among the shoppers in Belfast City Centre. Or at least, he told himself it was the wind causing the tears. Was it sissy-ish to be crying over his recently deceased twelve-year relationship? Exes were never worth it. That was why they were exes in the first place.

You're seeing him?

No, it's more complicated than that.

In what way? What's going on, Sonya?

Ben and Sonya's argument, or what little he had heard of it before he left Robinsons, played in his head.

Ben. What the fuck did Ben have that he didn't? What could that bastard offer Sonya that he couldn't? An ugly little voice shouted its word in his mind: Ben was perfectly formed. He wasn't a freak of nature; no parasitic twin had lurked in *his* abdominal cavity for the last thirty-three years. He sniffed and wiped the tears on the back of his hand, then wiped his hand on his trouser leg.

Castle Lane turned into Cornmarket. Beyond Cornmarket lay Victoria Square. The notion to go and see a film, instead of heading home alone and miserable, had been a sudden and appealing one. A mega bucket of popcorn and a massive tub of ice cream to keep him company. He would fill the baggy loose post-surgery skin on his gut with comfort cravings; a belly full of junk food instead of a belly full of parasitic brother.

As he turned into Cornmarket, close to where the old Woolworths store had been in his boyhood, he froze. Instead of the modern-day department store Dunnes, he visualised a stone tower, with a wooden platform in front, on which stood a gallows. Market House at Cornmarket had been the site of hangings in Belfast for many centuries. Henry Joy McCracken had been one of the more famous examples. As commander of the United Irishmen, he had led a group of mainly Ulster Scots rebels in a battle against the Crown forces in Antrim. He had been captured after hiding out on Cavehill for a month and had been hanged in 1798.

Cavehill had been a hiding spot for another, long before McCracken. Beollan and his family had hidden there too. As he had been captured and put to death by fire, a witch had been born: his daughter, Failenn.

Matthew stopped dead in his tracks, staring open mouthed at the site of the former gallows. But this wasn't the eighteenth century. This was an earlier time. Medieval Belfast, long before it was Belfast. *Béal Feirste*, the Gaelic name meaning Mouth of the Sandbank, or Crossing of the River. He was seeing fourteenth century Béal Feirste imposed over modern day Belfast city centre, like a double negative on an old camera roll.

Had a gallows stood there for many centuries before it became the famous one in the seventeenth century, known on the location of Cornmarket? He was no historian. But his eyes didn't deceive him. He was seeing another vision of medieval life, superimposed over modern day Belfast. The twenty-first century buildings faded until only the medieval surroundings remained, as if he was actually there.

He turned back to the gallows. Plain as day, he could see a man hanging by his neck from the gallows, strung up and in his final throes. It wasn't just any man. This was Aymer, his counterpart from medieval Ireland. Aymer's face was beetroot purple as the rope trapped all the blood in his head.

While still barely alive, Aymer was cut down, gasping for breath, and tethered to a wooden rack, that resembled a wooden lattice made of branches tied tightly together and held at a forty-five degree angle. A small crowd gathered, standing around Matthew, all of them watching the gallows. Two soldiers, wearing the yellow tunics with red lions of Edward Bruce's army, stretched Aymer's arms and legs wide and fastened his wrists and ankles to the wooden frame with ropes. Had this really happened in history; had this been how Aymer had met his end? He couldn't say, though he was thankful to be watching as an outsider this time, and not seeing the vision through Aymer's own eyes.

Come to think of it, why was he witnessing this vision as an outsider? He had seen other visions of Aymer's life through his own eyes.

He had no time to ponder the difference; an executioner appeared behind Aymer. The man was also a Scottish soldier in the yellow and red colours of Edward Bruce's army. The executioner hooked an axe inside the fabric of Aymer's linen tunic and cut upwards, then discarded the torn garment in two halves. Aymer's chin dropped forward onto his bare chest. He stood rooted in shock. Were they going to chop off his head? His limbs? Hanged, then drawn and quartered?

Worse. Matthew stood frozen as the soldier pierced Aymer's abdomen with a dagger and began to tear upwards. A wet, squelching emanated as blood and viscera spilled out; his medieval counterpart's eyes bulged and mouth gaped as his head shot upwards off his chest with the pain of disembowelment while he remained alive. The Scottish soldier replaced the dagger with the axe and wet squelching gave way to a cracking sound as Aymer's bones were hacked apart. As much as he didn't want to watch, he couldn't close his eyes against the horror of Aymer's fate.

The executioner set the axe aside, smeared burgundy red with blood and scraps of flesh that slid along its haft. He loomed over Aymer's exposed innards, peeling flesh curtains of skin to either side. Slippery organs and long, glistening intestines dripped between the wooden branches of the angled frame as the executioner reached into Aymer's body cavity.

"In the time of Pluto's return, in the year of 20 and 23, when the moon is in conjunction with Saturn, balance will be restored. The conjunction of two enemies, brothers in war, has begun," said a woman's voice behind Matthew on the wind.

He recognised the voice and spun around. Failenn, stood behind him. With a teasing smirk, she breezed past him, raising the hairs on the back of his neck as an icy chill swept over his body.

The witch approached Aymer's ruined body. The Scottish soldiers and crowd of peasants didn't see her, as though she was a ghost. Indeed, Matthew noted, she had a faint silvery outline around her; the only giveaway that she was a ghost in the vision, as her body appeared as solid as the soldiers in the scene of Béal Feirste.

Failenn emerged from Aymer's open torso with an arm outstretched towards Matthew. Sitting snugly in her palm was a plum-coloured flesh ball the size of a grapefruit. Stringy sinew trailed from the fleshy mass, along with dangling arteries that hung like tentacles. Like the witch, the fleshy ball had a faint silvery outline. He understood. It was also a ghost. Medieval Aymer didn't have a parasitic twin like he did. The witch, who was able to transport her consciousness, her ghost, through time had taken the soul of his parasitic twin with her this time to show a connection between him, and Aymer of the past.

As Failenn approached him, he saw two eyes blink open inside the ghastly mass and a gash opened below, as a mouth with crooked nubs of teeth.

"Veniam ad vos," said the fleshy mass, in unison with the witch.

Both hands flew to his temples as he screamed. The grisly image of blood-splattered soldiers, Aymer's murdered body, Failenn and the parasitic twin in medieval Béal Feirste disappeared in the blink of an eye. His cry echoed across modern day Cornmarket and all around, shoppers and tourists in the middle of Belfast turned and stared, as if he was crazy.

Maybe he was. "I'm going mad." He breathed in rattling gasps, his saliva thick in his throat. "I'm being driven insane. Failenn, why are you doing this?"

No answer, not even a sign. He looked to the sky. Not a seagull in sight, not even one sent to taunt him, or watch over him.

His eyes stayed on the looming grey clouds, regardless. "Where is this going to end? I'm no threat to you. Am I ?"

It would end with someone's death. He was sure of it. He couldn't change fate. It was his destiny to either fight or die. The witch Failenn, and the soldier Colbyn, were set on their revenge and he could do nothing to change their minds. They had waited for seven hundred and eight years. Twenty-twenty three. A medieval *mea culpa* was coming for him, whether he knew why, or not.

CHAPTER TWENTY-FOUR

Fires ravaged the countryside. Pyres made of timber from houses and churches spiralled up and out across the North channel. Some of the fires raged with such intensity that stone melted: from churches, forts and even castles. Only one castle withstood the onslaught. Carraig Fhearghais Castle was protected by its position on a high, basalt rock, repelling most attacks, and for now, the castle remained untouched. The seagull swooped inland. The battle was elsewhere.

The Scottish forces of Edward Bruce, aided by Irish Chiefs who were committed to the Scottish cause of repelling the English from Irish shores, ravaged the land. After Edward Bruce had landed at Latharna and moved on to Carraig Fhearghais in May of that year in 300 galleys, his 6000 followers had turned inland, putting English settlers to the sword, even women, children and the old.

A sense of excitement at the chaos in the countryside below filled the consciousness inside the seagull. Where did the feeling come from? Not his, Matthew's, consciousness. No; the emotions belonged to Failenn. The witch, controlling the bird, also dictated the mood to him as an interloper witnessing the scenes beneath.

The 26th of May in the year of 1315. It was a sign, an omen, from the Graceful Goddess of the Lunar Light that she would avenge Failenn's beloved father, Beollan, from the local heathens who had torched him on Beann Mhadagáin's Peak. That special date marked the day and month of Beollan's birth, fifty-four summers previously. He had been thirty when he had been murdered; the age she was now. The Scots would exact justice on the locals in Carraig Fhearghais who had committed a grievous sin against her. Sin. Sin, God of the Moon, would oversee the Graceful Goddess of the Lunar Light from on high, influencing the tides to bring more Scottish forces from Scotland, while the Earth Mother robbed the locals of their food. Famine was rife. The seagull flew lower.

Below, cavalry with swords, foot-soldiers with axes and archers moved northwards from Connaught, in the West of Ireland, towards Cúil Raithin, the modern-day town of Coleraine; a force of around 200 men. In the lead was a man wearing mail over his padded gambeson. He wore mail chausses over his padded hose leggings and a linen hauberk with a mail coif on his head. A squire carried his nasal helm, which he would need soon as battle beckoned. Failenn-seagull knew who he was by his arms: a red cross over a yellow shield. This was Richard de Burgh, the Red Earl of Ulster. The knights behind him were Irish chiefs of his province, Connaught. They rode north by day in aid of the English to rid the Scottish foe from their land and camped by night. Night after night, Sin shone his moonlight down on their camp as it moved ever closer to the English. Failenn wished the Graceful Goddess of the Lunar Light would strike down them down with fire, but the goddess had other plans for them. The witch hoped they would fail in their mission; she directed the seagull across the enemy forces and dropped a stream of scat over the soldiers. It missed the Red Earl, but struck lucky over the armour of his knights. Matthew's consciousness filled with the petty jubilation of the witch's triumph through their shared avian body.

The witch recognised another man: Edmund Butler, Justiciary of Ireland. The Red Earl and his army stopped as Butler's large reinforcement approached. The seagull landed on a nearby bough to listen.

"I have brought assistance. Two hundred good men, at your service," said Butler.

"We are grateful, but our troops are sufficient to repel the Scots. You may return home to defend Leinster. I and my vassals will overcome the enemy," said the Red Earl.

Richard de Burgh and his troops continued north into Ulster alone as Edmund Butler's reinforcements turned south. Failenn's happiness surged, flooding Matthew once more: Good, she thought, how encouraging that the local heathens had chosen to isolate themselves. Victory for the Scots would be assured, Failenn had no doubt.

Or maybe not? As they cut a path north through the wild countryside of Ulster, the Scots retreated in their wake, as the Red Earl's troops seized their provisions: bread; wine; armour; swords. Scottish camps were torched. The seagull flew on, and Matthew sensed Failenn's dismay.

Just as hope seemed lost, black smoke spiralled high into the heavens; the Scottish under Edward Bruce had sacked Cúil Raithin. They had burned the bridge over the River Bann, halting Richard de Burgh's pursuit. Failenn watched Edward Bruce crossing the River Bann with his men in a fleet of small wooden boats, curved at each end. The seagull veered left and saw Richard de Burgh change course in a southward direction, towards Tannybrake at Connor.

The bird's powerful wings propelled it onwards ahead of the Irish and Ulster troops. Towards the River Kell, near the village of Connor, in County Antrim, the Scottish had a plan. Once more, seagull Failenn alighted on a bough to listen.

Edward Bruce was recognisable by his coat of arms: yellow shield with red saltire and chief gules, and a royal azure lion within a white square in the top left corner. Astride his horse, he wore full armour mail chausses leggings and mail hauberk over his padded gambeson. Now that the battle at Cúil Raithin, present day Coleraine, was over he took off the great helm that protected his face and addressed his men. "The Irish Lords fight amongst themselves. Fedlimd O Conchobair and Ruaidri mac Cathal Ua Conchobair both withdrew support of the Red Earl as each believed I would support their position of king in

Connaught. There is discord as they each seek to defend the throne. Now is our time to attack the Red Earl – he has arrived at Connor."

Sir Phillip Mowbray, Keeper of Strivelyn Castle, modern day Stirling Castle, addressed the Scottish troops. Failenn knew him by his red shield, emblazoned with a white lion rearing up on its hind legs, coat of arms of the House of Mowbray. "I concur. We will draw them in, leave our banners flying in our camp. Then we will surprise them."

The Scottish forces moved south to Connor, ahead of the local forces. They set up camp and flew their yellow banners with red saltire. Edward Bruce led them in a wide circuit around the advancing local troops, using trees for cover, and closed the circle behind them.

The Scottish archers led the attack. Richard de Burgh evaded the arrows by sitting astride the left side of his horse as he charged forward to escape capture. He brought his longsword down chopping through the leather jerkins of men at arms and archers alike. Failenn recognised the Red Earl's cousin, William de Burgh; he was seized and taken prisoner, though Richard escaped.

The Red Earl led five men on horseback as they turned southwest and Failenn knew they rode back to Connaught. They knew the Irish countryside of their home better than the Scots, and left the latter trailing in pursuit. A band of thirty fugitives on horseback turned southeast. Matthew-seagull knew where they were destined, since the witch did, and followed them; soon the dark, imposing outline of Carraig Fhearghais Castle, on its rocky promontory came into view.

Failenn would have to warn Colbyn. But how could a seagull fly ahead of horses, galloping at full speed?

Matthew-seagull swooped lower towards the charred remains of Carraig Fhearghais town. Colbyn was one of a hundred men in the Scottish garrison in Carraig Fhearghais. In their padded wool and horsehair gambesons, covered with tunics showing Edward Bruce's yellow and red arms, she couldn't recognise him by his build. In their iron nasal helms along with padded coifs and arming caps obscuring their faces, she couldn't recognise him by face. Such was the life of men-at-arms. Her only consolation for her lover, and the garrison in general as her would-be victors, was that they outnumbered the fleeing fugitives by at least seventy men.

The garrison weren't on horseback. They were idle in their occupation of the town, and why not? The Scots not only outnumbered Henry Thrapston's men at Carraig Fhearghais, but were winning the war of their conquest in Ireland. So, when thirty men charged through the smoking remains in Carraig Fhearghais town, towards the raised portcullis of the castle, they were caught off guard. Archers lined the battlements, ready to attack any Scots if they tried to stop the fugitives from entering the castle and reinforcements stood at the machicolations, ready to pour boiling water or drop scorching salt on any would-be attackers. The Scottish garrison fell back. The seagull fell back. Carraig Fhearghais Castle, the charred town, Henry Thrapston's defenders, Scottish attackers; they all became one white haze as the witch pulled her gift from the feeble mind of the seagull and Matthew detached.

***

Matthew, whose mind had been inside Failenn, whose mind had been inside the bird, rocked backwards as metaphysical separated from physical. His eyes hurt with the strain, the bridge of his nose hurt with an unearthly pressure and his chest felt constricted as though it was expunged of air. Was he getting enough oxygen to his brain? Maybe not. His body had been taken, against his will, on a journey through time; an evil, unnatural one. But he was back now. Back with more information from the past. Like the Irish, English and Scottish soldiers of yesteryear, he was gearing up for a fight and had to equip himself. He was now Matthew, man-at-arms in a psychic fight for not only his earthly life, but for that of his immortal soul.

CHAPTER TWENTY-FIVE

Matthew looked down at the sketch he had doodled on his clipboard: a witch dangling from a hangman's noose, a seagull pecking out her eyes. His subconscious morbid fixation was bleeding into daily life; he needed distraction. Work was sufficient distraction. One thing Sonya had been right about was that work was a good focus for him; at least in terms of disciplining his mind.

The door opened and his colleague, Niall, peered around it. "There's a problem over at the holding pen. The new supervisor has gone to call the OV over in Scotland who checked the animals."

"What do you need me to do?" He crumpled the witch sketch and shoved it in his pocket, his clipboard ready with blank forms.

Niall dropped his clipboard on the table and set his torch beside it. "Just to take over as my shift is finished. Only wanted to give you a heads up for the handover, that's all."

"What's the new boss like?"

"Seems dead on." Niall nodded in the direction of the holding pen. "All you need to do with this lot is wait with the keeper until the new boss gets back with word from the vet."

He headed outside with his clipboard and torch. The keeper waited by the disembarkation gate, his eyes downcast. He approached the man. "Alright there? I'm Matthew the Duty Portal Inspector. I understand my supervisor is calling the OV? What's the problem?"

The keeper shook his head. "I can't say how this happened, I assure you it has never happened before. I checked all the tags before departure myself."

Matthew shone his torch into the holding pen and focused the beam on the nearest Angus cow. The button tags attached to the animal's ear showed its individual ID number and export tag. He froze. Instead of showing the ISO code number of 826 to indicate that it came from Scotland, the tag number 708 was displayed instead. He shone his beam on the next animal, and the one after that. They all had the ISO code 708 instead of 826.

Seven hundred and eight: the number of years connecting 1315 to 2023. Past to present. A witch using blood magic and runic symbols talking of spiritual awakenment, danger and anguish, birth and liberation of the soul. Revenge, the law of karma.

Revenge from a medieval past in the year 1315 to be wreaked on an innocent bystander caught up in the psychic turbulence in the year 2023. He was the innocent bystander.

He needed to snap out of it: focus on work, not on the supernatural. "What was the country of origin?"

"Scotland. They're from Perth. All the ISO codes read 826 when we embarked at Ayr this morning, I swear on my life," said the keeper.

Witchcraft and skulduggery. "I believe you. But we'll need it verified by the Official Veterinarian before they can disembark. The paperwork needs to be straight."

The new supervisor stepped out of the office. As he strode towards Matthew and the keeper, he couldn't help but stare at his new boss. The tall man, with dark hair and beard, sculpted jaw and broad shoulders, was none other than Ben, Sonya's new lover.

"You," he spluttered. Spit landed on his clipboard and he wiped it off with his sleeve. "You're the new supervisor?"

Ben ignored him and addressed the keeper. "I've had the confirmation from the OV that you need. The animals are cleared for disembarkation. He couldn't say what the mix up with the tags was, regarding the GB code being displayed as 708 instead of 826, but we'll put it down to a minor processing error."

The keeper smiled with relief. "You don't know how grateful I am for this. You saved my bacon. I might've been axed for that cock-up. I owe you one. If you need me, just call, Ben."

Call, Ben.
Colbyn.

Matthew glared at the keeper. "What did you just call him? Did you just say Colbyn?"

The keeper, and his new supervisor, glared at him in return.

"I said he could call me if he needs me. I owe him a big one." The keeper smacked his new boss on the upper back and they both grinned.

"No, you called him 'Colbyn'. I heard you." He pointed at his boss. "What's your name, and no more lies. I've had enough from both you, and Sonya. No games."

"I've already told you, my name's Ben." His boss raised an eyebrow as he looked from Matthew to the keeper and back to Matthew.

"Are you sure it isn't Colbyn?" He continued pointing at him.

"If I said my name's Ben, then it's Ben – and I don't like you pointing at me. My name's no more Colbyn than I thought yours was Andrew when I met you in Robinson's," said his boss.

He lowered his finger, but not his angry glare. "Is Ben short for anything?"

The muscles in his boss's chiselled cheeks tautened. "Not Colbyn, if that's what you're implying. Why don't you tell me what you're getting at here, mate? You're obviously mixing me up with someone else. Who's this Colbyn you're on about?"

Colbyn. It made his blood run cold.

The keeper snorted with laughter. "He's thinking of Corbyn, the one who was leader of the Labour Party – your man, Jeremy Corbyn. Beard's the wrong colour mate and he's about three decades too young."

The keeper and his boss guffawed, but he wasn't fazed: no distractions.

Stay focused.

Colbyn.

Colbyn. A medieval Scottish soldier, with a vendetta against the Anglo-Irish in Carrickfergus back in 1315.

"Ben must be your nickname. Colbyn's the name. Or Col, if you prefer?" He grinned at Ben and watched his toothy white smile fade.

"What planet are you on?" said Ben.

"He clearly has something against your name," said the keeper.

White zigzags swum before Matthew's eyes. He felt clammy, his head spinning. What was happening to him, to his life – to his world?

All that he knew was different and unsafe. He too felt different, and unsafe. They were both in on it; trying to trick him by pretending they knew nothing of his boss' real name, Colbyn.

"What's going on here?" He took a step back from Ben, though kept his eyes on him, as the enemy. "Where's Failenn? Bring the witch out. Or is it Sonya? Is she the one bewitching you? Is she behind all this?"

"Matthew, calm down," said Ben.

He took another step backwards. "That's it, isn't it? Sonya put you up to this. Both of you are in on it and Failenn's helping you. Failenn has you both bewitched."

"Who is Failenn?"

"Don't play dumb with me." He backed up against the nearest portacabin, feeling safety in the metal wall behind him. "Just tell me what your game is. First you steal Sonya away from me, and now you're my boss? Tell me your name right now, or I'll report you. You'll be hearing from my union rep!"

151

Too much. Just taking the effing piss. He shook his head as he crept further away from Ben, though not taking his eyes off the enemy for even a moment.

Ben put both hands up in an appeasing gesture. "I understand there's a lot going on for you, I get that. Why don't you take a break and—"

"If you tell me to go and see a shrink, I will seriously deck you one, even if you are my boss – mate."

Matthew marched back to his portacabin and clicked the button of the kettle with maybe more anger than he had intended. Fucking Ben. He wouldn't give him the satisfaction of walking off the job, going to see a shrink, or letting the bastard drive him crazy. It was his job and he'd been there longer than the homewrecker, job-stealer. He wouldn't let Colbyn trick him by pretending to be Mr. Nice Guy. He was the enemy. So be it. If a fight was coming, he would be prepared. Payback was best served cold.

CHAPTER TWENTY-SIX

He wasn't perfect. He was far from perfect. He knew this. After his motivational pep talk to himself about wanting to give his new supervisor payback, Matthew again found himself in the doldrums. Gary had been a saviour, meeting him for a pub lunch at short notice, and he had off-loaded. Now what did he have to wash down the three pints of Stella with? Bitter saliva swirled in his mouth at the thought of going home to a dark, empty house. Where was Sonya crashing now anyway; where did that *sleekit* bastard, Ben, live anyway? Probably over in Ballyhackamore, or even more posh, in Malone. Maybe the fucker was even born with a silver spoon in his mouth, for all Matthew knew? Born into wealth, guided by a witch's power from beyond the grave.

As he pulled up in front of his house, he saw that the bedroom light was on. He definitely hadn't left it on earlier that morning; his frugal nature made sure he always did a sweep of the house turning off all lights and switching off power sockets before heading out to work. What had Sonya come home for? She had taken all her clothes, and Jessie too. Had she come back for Failenn's urn?

He hurried upstairs and pushed the bedroom door open. Sonya's clothes were spread across the double bed, her overnight bag lying empty on the floor by the window. The shower hissed and steam swirled out from behind the half-open ensuite bathroom door. The tightness in his chest dissipated. Had Sonya come home to stay? If she'd had a fight with Ben, and was back to make amends, he was willing to listen and forgive her, within reason. He pushed the ensuite door open.

Behind the opaque glass door, a figure stood showering. His heart, which had softened only moments before, hardened again as he saw a naked male torso through the screen, and not Sonya. The shower stopped and in a puff of hot steam that assaulted his eyes and nose, Ben stepped out onto the bathroom rug. His taut physique dripped unwelcome droplets of water all over the floor and his irritatingly handsome face rumpled in confusion.

"Matthew, you're back."

Was this fella for real? "Of course I'm fucking back, I live here. What are *you* doing here?"

"Sonya has invited me to stay. She said you were going to leave."

"Oh, she did, did she?" He forced a theatrical, derisive guffaw. "Did the pair of you think you could just drive me out, eh?"

Ben, reached for a towel slung over the shower panel and began drying himself, then wrapped it around his well-toned midriff. As he slapped cologne on his face, he didn't take his eyes off Matthew. "Why don't we discuss this over a coffee?"

What a fucking *tube*. Not only was Ben completely at ease and unashamed that he had just got out of the shower in front of his junior employee, someone he barely knew, but he was unapologetic too. "You're shitting me, right?"

Ben sauntered past him, out of the ensuite, with a smile on his face. He had no choice but to follow him into the bedroom, in a cloud of his stinking cologne. Ben proceeded to strip off his towel and put on boxers, jeans and a t-shirt from neatly stacked piles that had already been arranged in the bedside drawers. Unfucking-believeable. As if in response to Ben's toned physique being brazenly flaunted in front of him, his stitches itched; his hand jumped to his waistband to scratch the healing skin. He, and his damaged-goods body had been dumped in favour of *Mr. Perfect* and his nauseatingly sculpted form.

"Sonya's downstairs brewing some Kenyan roast already." Ben inhaled, his muscular, hairy chest expanding. "Ah, that smells good."

Aye, the smell of his ex-girlfriend being made into a kitchen wench by some handsome bell-end who didn't love anyone but himself. He held his tongue. This wanker was still his boss; for the time being anyway.

Flying off the handle wouldn't do either of them any good. It was time for negotiations.

As he trailed downstairs behind Ben, thoughts of kicking him down the stairs crossed his mind. How satisfying that would be. They entered the kitchen and Ben swooped across and kissed Sonya on the lips; a quick peck.

"Oi, back off mate, you're forgetting whose woman that is – and whose house you're in." He grabbed Ben by his shoulder and yanked him away from her.

"Matty!" Her face was beetroot. "Don't be such a dick."

"*Me* being a dick?" He spun on the spot, calming himself. "Ack, piss off!"

Ben offered a mug of black coffee. He was tempted to smack it away but wouldn't give him the pleasure; he snatched it from Ben and cupped both hands around it. It was *his* mug in *his* house. But how did the bastard know he liked his coffee strong and black?

"Listen Matthew, it's clear we have some things to sort out. Sonya and I both know you've been through the ringer over these past few months."

The ringer. He blanched. What would that bastard know of anything?

"You've just got back into work after your surgery, and then there's me working as your new supervisor to contend with, as well as things between you and Sonya–"

"Things between Sonya and me are nothing the fuck to do with you. Why are you even here?" He faced Sonya. "Who are you with, me or him?"

Her eyes and mouth widened. "Well, it shouldn't be like that, really."

"Yes, it should. Choose," he said.

Sonya bit her bottom lip and turned to Ben, doe-eyed.

"Fine. You choose him. But what about me. Half the mortgage on this house is mine."

"Yeah, but it's co-ownership, Matty. Ben could pay the part that's rent, you know, like a tenant." She sucked in a deep breath. "I want him to stay."

"If he stays, I go." He set his coffee mug down with a thunk.

"You don't have to. There's the spare room–"

"Spare room? I don't believe my fucking ears."

He stomped back upstairs, grabbed Sonya's overnight bag on the floor and emptied his clothes out of drawers into it. He had never been so insulted in all his life. Where would he stay? His thoughts raced quickly as he ruled each one out. He hadn't patched things up with his parents after their tiff, so he couldn't go there. As he marched back downstairs, Matthew punched Gary's number into his phone.

CHAPTER TWENTY-SEVEN

Tears dripped everywhere: on Gary's carpet, on the coffee table, all over the sofa. Matthew snivelled and blew his nose into the last tissue in the box.

"It's good of you and Katie to let me stay. It's not going to wake up the kiddos, is it?"

Gary waved his concerns away. "They're grand. They'll be happy to have someone new to play with. They see you as their Uncle Matt."

He sniffed the last of his tears away. He couldn't go to pieces over Sonya and Ben; they weren't worth it.

Katie appeared in the living room doorway. She shut it quietly and walked across to Gary, taking a seat beside him on the sofa. "How're you doing Matt?"

"Not brilliant, as you can see. I feel like everything has gone pear-shaped since my operation. I've lost Sonya to some arsehole who turns out to be my new boss. On top of that, I feel like I'm losing my mind. All these dreams of medieval Carrickfergus and a witch, and two soldiers – one on the Scottish side, one on the Anglo-Irish side. It's taking over my life. It's like I'm going insane."

"It makes perfect sense to me," said Katie. "Witches in dreams symbolise healing. You started to dream of her around the time your twin brother began getting restless in your body. It was around the time the pain started to intensify, wasn't it?"

He gave a solemn nod.

"Then the witch appearing to you night after night was your subconscious telling you that you were undergoing a transformation. You felt powerless, but she was telling you to look within and discover that you have the ability and wisdom to face your fears and conquer them."

"It was more than a dream. I saw her in the holding pen at work hiding behind a shipment of Scottish cattle. And what about the urn?" He reached into Sonya's overnight bag and brought out the small clay vessel covered in occult runes. He handed it to Katie, satisfied when he saw her flinch before taking it from him.

Katie turned it round and round, inspecting it. "Is this the one that Sonya gave you? She mentioned something when we talked on the phone, about getting you a present after your operation."

"She got it from her dig in Carrickfergus. She meant for it to cheer me up, but it disturbed me. It has occult powers — it was used in a necromancy ritual to secure a victory for Edward Bruce's army."

Katie and Gary were wide-eyed in their silence.

"I think Sonya meant well, but it wasn't a good present for you. I know she intended it as an object of healing, but I think it has done more subconscious damage to your psyche than what you could cope with. I mean, the burden of your operation alone was a lot for most people to bear — but the strain of all this loaded symbolic imagery on top of it is not anything you need."

He frowned. "What do you mean by loaded symbolic imagery?"

Katie spun the pot around and pointed to a triangular rune that pointed left, resembling a mathematical less-than symbol. "This sign has had an unfortunate negative effect on your subconscious self. It has made you feel inferior, like less than the man you are, as a result of carrying your twin brother in your body for thirty-three years."

"Aye, that's because it looks like a less-than symbol in maths. There's no loaded symbolic mystery with that one. Less than equals inferior."

A faint blush appeared on Katie's cheeks. She bristled but continued. "See this one here? It looks like a capital D and stands for death. That word had been embedded in your mind as a lingering fear and guilt that you inadvertently killed your twin brother, simply by having that operation to separate you both."

He pointed at the rune shaped like a D. "The witch Failenn said that rune represented danger and anguish and marked the Scottish soldier's departure from this world. She also said that in numerology it marked the start of a spiritual journey and therefore it presented as the number zero."

"See what I mean? That witch was your dream-self sending the same message to you – only instead of a Scottish soldier, it was your twin brother departing the world, and the associated guilt you felt with that." Katie turned the urn around and pointed to another symbol, that looked like a capital B, if written in straight lines, like two triangles joined together. "This B stands for birth. A stillbirth, in a way, of your brother."

He gulped. "The witch said that all three of these runes had meanings in numerology as well. The less-than triangle stood for the number 7. The capital D shaped rune stood for a 0 and the capital B stood for the number 8. Seven hundred and eight years brings us from the medieval into the present – right now in the year 2023.

Katie and Gary looked pale; or maybe it was the dim lamplight in their living room.

"Do you know the name of the Scottish soldier in my dreams? His name was Colbyn. My new boss, who incidentally is now shagging my ex-girlfriend, is called Ben. Get it? Ben? Colbyn? One of the cattle keepers even said 'just call, Ben'. Colbyn. Coincidence? Or something more?"

"I dunno, Matt. That's a bit of a stretch." Gary's forehead rumpled. "Is his name really Ben, or Colbyn?"

"Well, he insists his name is Ben, but I know he's lying."

Gary stared benignly at him and said nothing more.

He turned the urn round and round in his palm, staring at it, as though it would reveal hidden knowledge; though nothing came to mind. "There's something that has been bugging me too. I'm starting to think that Ben is a reincarnation of medieval Colbyn, the Scottish soldier wanting revenge."

Gary and Katie glanced at each other, then turned back to face him.

"Look, I know how it sounds, but hear me out. You're my best mate. Have you ever known me to be irrational, or to believe in anything supernatural?"

Gary shook his head. "You're the biggest atheist I know."

"Exactly. So, what would it take for me to start believing in strange occult shit and get completely spooked?" he continued.

Gary puckered his lips. "Alright mate. You've got my attention."

He gave a satisfied smile. "I suspect that he wants revenge on the people who killed him – and that something in the past happened to stop him from doing that during his lifetime. All the visions I've seen so far, starting in 1315 when Edward Bruce's army invaded, are playing out a story. All three of them – the Scottish soldier, Colbyn, the Anglo-Irish soldier, Aymer, and the witch, Failenn – I've been seeing their stories, their lives in medieval Carrickfergus."

"Well, that makes sense, doesn't it? Sonya's working on a new dig in Carrick, isn't she?" said Katie, a hopeful glint in her eyes.

He shook his head. "I'm not dreaming these things up because my ex-girlfriend is working on a dig in that town, if that's what you're getting at."

Katie flushed. "Sorry, Matt. I wasn't implying that."

He exhaled and allowed his body to relax. "No, I'm sorry. I've been defensive because I feel like nobody believes me and everyone is out to attack me. These people in the past, and now Sonya and my parents on top of that."

"We do believe you, mate. It's just that it sounds so…" Gary trailed off as he composed his thoughts, "amazing, you know. Incredible."

Katie cut Gary off. "Where do you come into the story, Matt?"

"See that's the thing I've been wondering myself. When I see the visions of witch Failenn and the soldier Colbyn, it's as though I'm watching from the outside, like I'm a ghost in the room, whereas the visions with Aymer are is like I'm seeing directly through his eyes. Well, all except for one vision of Aymer's death where I was seeing it from the outside because Failenn was showing it to me as though to taunt me. But the other visions of Aymer's life, when I saw everything through his eyes, makes me think that I actually *was* Aymer in a past life."

Gary and Katie listened without interrupting. He was pleased at their attentiveness; maybe they were starting to believe him.

"In one of Failenn's visions, I saw how her father died. He was murdered by the townsfolk of Carrickfergus. They chased him up onto Cavehill and burned him alive. It's obvious the witch wants revenge against the people who did that – and apparently there are sixteen of them."

"Do you think Aymer was one of those people?" said Gary.

"Maybe, though I didn't see him among the townspeople who chased her father," he answered.

Gary looked puzzled. "If he killed her dad – and the Scottish soldier, then that would make sense why she wants revenge on you, wouldn't it?"

He inhaled. "I wish I knew. I haven't seen enough visions of the past to know for sure."

Katie looked pensive. "You know, I'm just thinking back to what you said before about Failenn's prophecy of 708 years after the year 1315. There's no way that Ben today could be a reincarnation of medieval Colbyn. The dates wouldn't work. It would have to be a baby born this year in 2023 for her foretelling to work, wouldn't it?"

A baby born this year. It was as though a switch had been flicked on in Matthew's brain. He looked down at the urn resting in his cupped palms, which sat on top of the sagging bulge of his stretched stomach; a gut that had held a parasitic lifeform, a foetus-in-foetu, in his abdominal cavity.

Movement behind Katie and Gary on the sofa drew his eye. He jerked his head upwards to the living room mirror on the far wall behind them. Failenn's reflection appeared as though she stood in the room, although the witch hadn't materialised in person; only her form in the mirror. Her green eyes were locked on him, a sneer fixed on her face.

He watched in horror as the witch held the fleshy mass of his parasitic twin in her left hand, stroking it like it was a pet with her right hand. Tendrils of sinew and stringy arteries began stretching from the fleshy mass. They began to thicken, filling with flesh as though stems cells were causing limb buds to sprout. From the stumpy limbs, arms and legs began to grow; fingers and toes erupted from the tips of each of the four limbs. A nub on top sprouted into a head. As the mass in the mirror reflection grew bigger, Failenn let it roll out of her palm, where it dropped to the floor and continued growing. The raw-meat coloured flesh grew paler until Matthew saw a Caucasian human form stand upright, lithe and muscular. He had black hair, and a black beard, and a devilish glint in his eyes to match his devastatingly handsome, grinning face. Medieval Colbyn – modern Ben – stood next to the witch.

"No," he gasped. His right hand jumped to his chest, steadying his hammering heart.

There was no more doubt in his mind. Colbyn, Ben and his parasitic twin were, somehow, all the same person.

"Yes," said mirror-reflection Failenn. "Believe it. It is done. By the Grace of the Lunar Goddess, it is done."

"No," he shrieked. "It can't be. This is too much. It's sick."

"He's your brother now, your fates are forever intertwined."

"No!" He dropped his head to his knees, balling into a foetal position. The urn dropped out of his hand and rolled on the carpet.

"Matt, what's going on? Who are you talking to?" said Gary.

"He was looking at the mirror, honey. Something scared him in the mirror," said Katie.

He heard their voices, but they couldn't help him. No one could help him. This was a metaphysical fight, with forces much stronger than him. But he would get stronger. He would find out what role Aymer had to play in the past, and undo the damage from his previous life, to save his life in the present.

CHAPTER TWENTY-EIGHT

Yule drew near. The evenings were getting darker earlier in the day and the nights longer and colder. Samhain had come and gone without any harvest to speak of, for famine had ravaged the land. Both wood and lea had been put to torch by the Scots. Barn and church, crop and stead; all had been fired across the land.

Carraig Fhearghais Castle's supplies of wheat, corn, oats and wine had dwindled to almost nothing. What he would have given for swan. Swan had not been on the castle menu for the longest time; close to a year. No feasting, no merriment, only war and hunger.

Christmas approached, but how many would see the yuletide celebrations? No roast beef, pudding and pies this year, though his mouth watered at distant memories, when the town wasn't at war. This year there would be no mummers acting out the traditional stories of St. Stephen's Day. There would be no loaf of barn brack thrown out to ward off hunger for the year. The last of the corn shipments from Dubh Linn, that had slipped through despite attempts to divert it by the Scots, was a distant memory. Famine and pestilence besieged the land; most peasants had died of the dreaded plague that followed many months of torrential rain, or had turned into creatures of myth, wandering the swamps, pale and wan, covered in boils. Some said mothers ate their babes, men feasted on the carcasses of horses that had fallen by the wayside. Could such tales have any truth? He knew not, holed up in the castle keep, as he was, protected from plague; but not an empty stomach. What was worse than starvation? The Scottish army was worse. Bad tidings had reached them, through their scouts. Worse was coming; there were rumblings of Bruce's army returning to Ulster.

But for now, Aymer focused on his hunger, distracting as it was. How long since he had eaten a proper meal? He imagined a tender, juicy piece of swan breast as he looked down at the scrap of leather hide that lay, a miserable sight, on his pewter plate. He had already sheared the fur off the blanket when he had taken it from the banquet hall, and had sliced it into twelve squares to share with the other soldiers.

"Aymer, take this. There is scant nourishment to be had from it, but more than you will derive from chewing that scrap of hide."

He looked down at the corner of spiced bread that had been dropped on his plate. It was hard as a rock, stale for perhaps a month, maybe more. A rat, or other vermin had chewed holes in it. He used his back teeth to crunch the solid piece.

Chewing hides and stale hunks of bread; not a noble task. The meaning of his name, Aymer, had never been further from the truth. Aymer: noble or famous. There was nothing noble about it, though maybe, with time, the plight of the soldiers trapped inside the castle would become famous across the land. Their stand against the Scottish would be known, once they became the victors and expelled the enemy from their land.

The door to the entry floor of the keep opened, casting a cold chill across the room; Aymer peered over the heads of the other starving soldiers huddled around the bare wooden table, to see one of their scouts enter. He stopped chewing the stale scrap of bread, eager to hear news.

"What tidings are there of the Scottish in Dundalk?" he asked.

The scout steadied himself with a hand on the table, catching his breath. "Edward Bruce defeated the Lord of Trim at Dundalk."

"It can't be true," he argued. "Lord Mortimer had a strong force."

"I'm afraid it's true. He was helped by De Lacy enemies of Mortimer. His forces moved on to Meath after that, Kildare too, ravaging everything in their path."

Aymer frowned. "But what of Edmund Butler? Richard De Burgh himself tasked the Lord Justiciary with guarding Connaught? I hear he moved to defend Meath?"

"Edward Bruce crossed paths with him near Anscoll. The English numbered a great many more than the Scots, but they were burdened by discord, and scattered."

"Scattered?" enquired another soldier.

"They fled. But not before taking two Scottish knights – Fergus of Androssan and Walter of Moray."

Aymer felt a rush of defiance, coursing through his body. "Is that not good news? I say it is. Good tidings are on our side yet, we mustn't despair. The famine that ravages this land will take the Scots too, especially if they are out of resources."

"But they have recruited a strong force of Galloglasses." The scout grew pale, a haunted look overcoming him. "I have never seen the like of such monstrous giants before, fearsome gaelic mercenaries, the worst of Scots and Irish combined. It was as though they were sent from the pit of hell itself."

Aymer imagined the hulking brutes, tall as a man plus half, and thick as tree-trunks, clad in the armour of knights and roaming the Irish countryside, an unstoppable force. He shivered.

He shook his head, a grim feeling seizing him. "Those are bad tidings. How long? Will they be here before Christmas?"

"They will. The Scots have depleted all of their supplies now. They're returning to Ulster. Greencastle has fallen. They'll be coming for Carraig Fhearghais next."

CHAPTER TWENTY-NINE

Matthew parked his car further down the street and waited. In the semi-darkness of the early morning, he watched for Sonya to leave for work. Both of them – Sonya and Ben – emerged a few moments later; he ground his teeth as he watched the smug couple get into Ben's car and drive away, resisting the urge to tail the smug git and rear-end him.

With the coast clear, he turned into the short driveway of the semi-detached house that he shared with Sonya. *His* driveway. His house, not Ben's. He and Sonya shared co-ownership of the house: part rent, part buy. She couldn't get rid of him so easily in favour of her new fancy-man; he had legal rights. Nobody would turf him out of the house that he part-owned, especially not some reincarnated medieval wanker. He fumed as he got out of his car.

Fight them in the present, as well as in the past. All of their fates were linked; but his destiny was his own. The future was his.

Out of the car, into the house. As the door shut behind him, he felt safe, cocooned within the protective space of his home comforts. This was his fortress. No, not a fortress; a castle.

Sonya wouldn't drive him out; neither would Ben.

Ben. He thought of the tall, handsome man who was both his boss and his ex's romantic partner. Could it really be his parasitic twin brother, 'born' into the world a mere month ago? Unless the ball of muscle mass, sinew and bone had magically grown into a fully developed adult human; one who could hold down a job and romance a lover, in a mere four weeks, such a notion was impossible. Yet that was what Failenn's reflection in Gary and Katie's mirror had shown him, in a diabolical display. Could witchcraft really have played a part in the rebirth of a medieval foe, now as his twin nemesis?

Or what about reincarnation? Supposing that Ben was the reincarnation of medieval Colbyn, born in the nineties as Matthew was, but that Failenn's presence had somehow 'activated' the dormant ghost within its twenty-first century human husk? That seemed more plausible than a parasitic twin, a mutant growth, suddenly sprouting arms, legs, a head and a conscience in a month, and not only that, but learning to talk and function in society.

The thought made him shudder. Whether medical-miracle or reincarnated wonder, either option gave him the creeps.

He locked the front door and barricaded it by putting the chain on it. Sonya had her own keys, of course, but she wouldn't be able to get in if his own keys were jammed in the lock from the inside and the safety chain was on. Next, he set about locking all the windows and the back kitchen door, jamming the spare set of keys in the handle to evade her attempt to try getting in from the back.

Solitude in his castle; he grinned to himself.

Carrying out his devious plan had worked up his appetite; and lucky for him, he had planned ahead. Unlike the normally bare cupboards, since both of them often forgot to pick up groceries, he had done an early morning supermarket run before waiting for the *sleekit* pair to leave for work. With only himself to cater for, he cooked a slap-up fry worthy of a king.

Yep, a king of his own castle. Holed up inside his kitchen-keep, protected from enemy invaders who meant him harm.

For crying out loud, medieval Aymer had really *turned his head*, dictating a script that was running from a part of his subconscious, of its own accord.

As he munched on his fry-up, he indulged his thoughts of his medieval past life. What could Aymer, Anglo-Irish soldier of Carrickfergus castle, have done to Failenn and Colbyn that was so bad it merited revenge 708 years later? In his vision of Failenn's bonfire, when Matthew had seen the townsfolk of Carrickfergus chase and attack her father, Beollan, and burn him alive, his past self – Aymer – had not been present. Or had he? Admittedly, he had not looked for

Aymer among the crowd; nor had he been shown the horrific murder through Aymer's eyes. It had been Failenn's memory, shown through the bonfire where her father had floated as a ghost in the flames.

Besides, even if Aymer had been one of the pursuers on Cavehill that fateful night, Failenn had been a girl, so Aymer would have been a boy. In 1315, when the adult witch had shown her psionic visions through the seagull, Failenn had been in her late twenties and Aymer in his mid-thirties at most.

No, he convinced himself, boy-Aymer could not have been part of the mob who had chased Beollan to Cavehill and burned him alive. He couldn't have, could he?

If he wasn't, then what might have been the witch's motivation for wanting revenge on him? Colbyn's grudge made more sense; maybe Aymer had killed him in battle, and he wanted revenge, though he had not yet seen any bloody fight between the pair, if it had indeed happened at all. Supposing they had fought, and Aymer had become the victor; Failenn helping Colbyn and his fellow Scots win their conquest in Ireland was not enough motivation to exact what seemed like a personal vendetta against Matthew and a few other Carrickfergus townsfolk – sixteen, according to the vision of the bonfire and her father, Beollan. If she had a grudge against sixteen Anglo-Irish townspeople in medieval Carrickfergus, and had cursed them all, did she intend to exact revenge on them all, starting with his past life self, Aymer?

He was sure he was missing something. There was still some key information from the past that explained why Failenn and Colbyn were pursuing him with such fury in a personal vendetta.

"Whatever you did, Aymer, it couldn't have been that bad – could it?" He listened to his own frightened voice dissipate into the still air of his living room.

Could it?

CHAPTER THIRTY

Adrenaline flooded Matthew's veins as Ben's car turned into the driveway. Sonya got out of the passenger side, her face lit up in laughter at something her loverboy had said. He opened the bedroom window and peered out, knowing that their happiness would turn to confusion, then outrage, once they realised that they had been locked out of the house.

Although he couldn't see them standing on the porch, as the front door was covered by a small roof, he heard the jangle of Sonya's keys as she fumbled with the lock.

"What the hell? Something's jamming it."

The note of panic in her voice made him snigger.

"He wouldn't have changed the locks, would he?" Ben's voice sounded gruff; he grinned imagining the bastard glowering at the keyhole.

"I wouldn't put it past him." Sonya huffed.

He felt a tremor of excitement.

"Oh my God. He must be inside. His key must be in the lock – that's what's blocking it."

A third voice, whiny and nasally joined them and the sound of a football being bounced on concrete. "Y'alright there love? Whassamatter?"

Tommy from next door. He smirked to himself. If there was to be any nosy bystander, it would be the knobhead teenager.

"We're alright, T. Away on inside your house now." Sonya sighed.

"Here, I can pick the lock if ya like. It's easy."

Wee fucker; did that mean Tommy the knob had been in their house before? He resisted the temptation to shout down at the tube.

"I don't need your help. Cheerio now, Tommy."

How he loved to hear the exasperation in her voice. Public humiliation for the win. A moment later, her flame-red hair appeared on the lawn and her eyes narrowed as she glared up at the open window. "Matthew, what the hell are you doing? Let us in."

He folded his arms on the windowsill and smirked down at her. "And what if I don't?"

She huffed. "Don't be a dick. Open the door and let us in so we can all talk about things."

"Why should I?" He leaned forward, looking down his nose at her. "So that you can take over *my* house with your unwanted lover, who legally has no right to be here at all."

Another sigh from Sonya. "Okay, fine. Ben can move his stuff out while we figure this out."

"Colbyn you mean, not Ben. Figure what out? You want your lover to share *my* house, and I don't. There's nothing to figure out."

Ben appeared next to Sonya on the grass, both his palms up in front of his face. "Listen, mate, if you just let me in, I'll grab my stuff and load it into the car. I swear to you, that's all I'll do."

"Aye right," he growled. "I wasn't born fucking yesterday. You'll get in here and I'll be forced to stay at Gary's again tonight."

"No, Matthew. He swears to you – I swear to you – he'll get his stuff and go. And then you and I can talk about this." Sonya's voice was pleading, a desperate look in her eye.

He waggled a finger out the window at Ben. "I know who you are. I'm not stupid. You're my brother. You're that thing that came out of me. I don't know exactly how Failenn did it, but she used witchcraft to help your stem cells to grow, didn't she? That's why you look as perfect as you do. But I know the truth. You're nothing more than my mutated parasitic twin, and now you want to live parasitically off me too – by taking my woman, a promotion I might have applied for, and now my house too."

Sonya and Ben were both quizzical as they turned to face each other. He saw his ex-girlfriend's face brighten, her mouth opening wide in glee as she turned back to him.

"You're absolutely right. Yes, Matthew, you're right. That's why I wanted Ben to live with us – because he's your brother. I really want the three of us to work this out. Matty, I have an idea. Why don't we come in and then we can, all three of us, talk this through like adults."

"I'm not falling for that." Spit flew from his mouth. "I wasn't born yesterday – unlike that bastard, who's only a few weeks old."

She looked at Ben, stepping from one foot to the other in impatience, then turned her face upwards to him at the bedroom window. "But he's your brother. Aren't you happy he isn't dead? I'm sure you always wanted to have a brother – and now you do."

"Brothers don't try to kill each other – and that mutated fucker wants me dead. Why don't you ask him, Sugar, what his real mission is?"

She rolled on the balls of her feet; he knew she was eager to end the impasse. But she was a fool.

"Matty, come on. He's your brother. Why would he want to harm you? You nurtured him in your body for thirty-three years. Doesn't that mean anything to you?"

Ben glared at her, a horrified expression coming over his face. She swiped a hand at him, silencing him before he could argue.

"Didn't you listen to a word I said about my visions of the past?" Matthew's voice grew louder. "He's Colbyn. I'm Aymer. We're enemies. From the way you're talking, I'm starting to suspect that you're Failenn."

"Who, the witch?" She shook her head with the animation of a toddler protesting innocence after a misdemeanour. "I'm just me – Sonya. I'm not a reincarnation of anyone, babe. You have to believe me."

"I believe you're in danger of possession. Only fools make themselves vulnerable to possession, and you're certainly acting an eejit when it comes to believing the bad guy – Ben here, or should I say, Colbyn – and not the man you supposedly loved for twelve years."

She stopped rocking on the balls of her feet and let them drop flat on the ground. "Matthew, there is no witch. All this talk of medieval sorcery is just a fantasy you dreamed up because of the pain of Ben here inside you. There is no witchcraft – he looks the way he does because of modern medicine and stem cell technology. Queen's University and the Royal Victoria hospital are world class, Matthew. The biology research is second to none elsewhere in the world. He's your brother, for crying out loud, have some compassion."

"Ha!" he shouted. "That's convenient. Expect me to believe that unlikely story?"

"Makes more sense than witchcraft, if that's what you're saying." Sonya huffed.

"Well, I'm not buying it. No modern medicine could make that bastard–" He paused, pointing at Ben, "–grow full-sized in just over a month. Only necromancy can do that."

She threw up her hands in anger. "And I thought you were an atheist! Fine, Matthew. Have it your way. Do you realise Ben has already met your mum and dad? We drove past them the other day and they stopped to chat when we pulled over. Sylvia and Gordon are so taken with him. They thought they had lost their baby when you absorbed him. Can you imagine how delighted they were to find out that he's alive after all these years, a son they never had?"

"You introduced that fucker to my mum and dad?"

He grabbed his hair on either temple and screamed. Sonya had gone too far; that was too big a betrayal. How could she have put his vulnerable, elderly parents in harm's way at the hands of a medieval enemy.

"If you ever bring that abomination near my mum and dad again, I'll have that bastard arrested. I'll call the police on you both!" he shrieked.

"Hey, watch it, you're going too far!" Ben protested, shaking a fist.

Sonya's face crumpled, a one-eighty from delight to frustration in three seconds flat. "Why are you being so difficult? I've honestly had it up to my neck with you this past month. I've tried to be supportive, but nothing gives with you Matty, not ever. You always have to have things your way."

His jaw dropped. "I don't believe what I'm hearing. Supportive? You cheat on me with this sleekit bastard, even when you knew he stole the promotion I wanted, and you endanger the lives of my parents by introducing him to them, and then you try to convince me that he's well meaning, just because he's my twin brother? I don't even know you anymore, Sonya."

Ben held his arms wide in defeat. "I'm the innocent party here. I thought Sonya was single when we started seeing each other a few weeks ago, so it wasn't like I was encouraging her to cheat. How was I to know you were cooped up in hospital recovering? As for your job – the position was advertised externally. How could I have known it was a promotion that you wanted? I applied for it, and I got the job fair and square. And you can't blame me if Sylvia and Gordon are taken with me."

"Mum and dad to you, what sort of son are you? No respect. I'm the proper son, you're just an abomination. You'll never be the real son!" he shouted.

"Matty, please. If you're reasonable, we can all find a solution. We can all be winners in this," Sonya whined.

"Shut up! I don't know you. All I know what it is you're after – and you're not going to win. You and Failenn, you've got it all worked out, don't you? Ben's not so innocent as you might think, Sugar. He has a plot against me with that medieval witch who made the urn."

Her face brightened. "Do you have the urn? Tony said you were going to drop it off to the site. He needs it back."

"Aye, because you stole it. You lied to me. You didn't take it off the spoil heap. You excavated it from where it was – in situ, to use your archaeological terminology – and you pocketed it to give it to me. Tell me this, Sonya. Are you in on the plot with Failenn and Colbyn?"

A red wave swept across her cheeks and forehead. "Babe, what the hell are you talking about? There *is* no witch, and I don't know who Colbyn is. I met Ben a month or so ago while you were recovering in hospital. I can't explain how your handsome brother grew out of that mass that came out of your operation – maybe it was super healing, or stem cells, or who knows? All I know is that there is no conspiracy against you, but you know what I think? Your mother backs me up about this too – you've taken on too much stress after your operation and it's causing you to be paranoid."

He ground his teeth. "Oh, so that's it. You and my mum think I'm ready for the funny farm."

Sonya sighed. "You aren't listening to me. You know what? You really confuse me sometimes, seriously. One minute you're all hardworking and focused and the biggest atheist I know who has his head on straight and the next minute you're babbling about odd dreams of witches and medieval soldiers and not making any sense."

"Alright fine. If you want logic, then let's be logical." He took a deep breath, composing his thoughts. "How did you meet mister hotshot here – and when?"

Her mouth puckered as she pondered the question. "Erm, let me think. It was at the Crown bar one evening, about a week after your operation."

"Hmph. That's rich. So, while I was all holed up in my sickbed you were out humping my so-called brother, this homewrecker here. That's just bloody typical!" He shook his head.

"Don't talk to me like I'm a whore." Sonya glowered at him. "I really don't like these changes in you at the moment. I'm trying to understand, I really am, but I need consistency myself – and who's supporting me? You're mum has been a gem, but honestly, I'm appreciating the short moments of respite that I get with Ben here. He's like you, but nicer, cooler, sexier. More fun. You want to know the truth? That's why I wanted to move him into the spare room. I thought it would help. I can't cope with everything these past couple of months, Matthew. I'm cracking up!"

Saliva flew out of her mouth on the last few words, and tears followed. He felt a jolt of shock in the pit of his stomach at seeing her so upset; he couldn't recall the last time she had cried.

A tear trickled out of the corner of his left eye, followed by a flow as salt water flooded. He wiped the stream off his left cheek, before poking a finger into the tear duct to stem the flow.

"*You're* cracking up? What about me? I'm the one who just had an operation to remove a parasite from my body, that happened to be my twin brother who had been living there for the past thirty-three years. Not only that but my girlfriend, and my parents, and my best mate and his wife all think I'm a loon because nobody believes me that my life – and my fate – are tied up with a medieval witch and a murderous soldier with a vendetta against me. Then, as if that wasn't the biggest kick in the teeth, my parasitic twin turns out to be the paranormal reincarnation of the medieval soldier seeking revenge on me, who comes along, steals my woman and takes the promotion that had my name written on it!"

His shrill voice echoed in his ears. When he heard his words laid out, piercing the air in their desperation, it sounded crazy. Absurd, and crazy. Yet it was all real, all too real, and happening to him. Why couldn't Sonya be more understanding of that?

She hiccoughed. "It's clear we're at an impasse here. What do you want me to say? If you're not going to let us – me – in so that we can talk about things, then I feel like we're at a dead end. What do you suggest we do?"

CHAPTER THIRTY-ONE

What do you suggest we do.

Hmph. As if that wasn't the biggest punch-in-the-gut question to add insult to injury.

What do you suggest we do? If only her words were hollow, a meaningless placation, but they weren't. She really meant it. She wanted to find a workable solution for all of them — all three of them. Him. Her. And the other — Ben. *Colbyn.*

"Fuck off, that's what I want you to do." Matthew muttered the words to himself as he dragged Ben's clothes out of the bedside drawers and over to the window. He knew he was being petulant, but he couldn't resist.

"Come back to the window, let's keep talking. We can work this out," she shouted.

"Work it out? Work *this* out."

He returned to the window with an armload of Ben's clothes. Shirts and trousers spread like parachutes all over the garden as he emptied his armload outside and his parasitic twin's eyes bulged in outrage. His reaction was incentive to continue; he proceeded to grab handfuls of Sonya's clothes out of the wardrobe and throw them into the garden.

"Matty stop, are you mad? This is going too far. Take your key out of the door and stop being a baby. Let me in!"

"I'm not a baby, your boyfriend is – he's the one who was only born mere weeks ago." He grinned as he chucked another load of Ben's clothes out the window.

"That's not fair. Lay off the insults, there's plenty of things I could say about you, but I'd rather be an adult about things," she whined.

"Cradle snatcher." He dumped her coats on her head.

"How can I help you when you won't help yourself? You're seriously your own worst enemy–"

"No," he shouted, cutting her off. "There's worse enemies – like a medieval witch and one of Edward Bruce's own vengeful foot soldiers. Try having them come after you and see how you would cope."

Movement at the far corner of the room caused a chill to trickle along his back. He spun around with a gasp, his heart hammering in his chest, in time to see a brown blur hurry across the landing and down the stairs.

He dashed out of the bedroom and looked over the bannister. His throat was bone-dry as he watched Failenn's back retreating down the stairs, her mousey brown hair flying behind her. The witch rushed towards the front door.

"No, Failenn, don't open that door!"

Too late. The witch unlocked the door and glided outside onto the front porch. He bounded downstairs after her, taking three steps at a time, but stumbled on the front doorstep, falling forward onto his knees. By the time he hauled himself to his feet and dashed outside into the garden, the witch had reached Sonya.

"Sugar, look out," he screamed.

Sonya and Ben both turned at the same time. Matthew was caught between fear at what Failenn would do to her, and relief that Sonya could see the witch too. In spite of everything: how she had cheated on him; all their arguments over the past few months, he still loved her.

"What's going on?" Sonya yelped, her terrified face fixed on Failenn.

The witch let out a shriek and lunged at her, her arms outstretched towards Sonya's throat. Sonya fell backwards with Failenn on top of her, throttling her. In the split second it took him to close the gap between himself and the women, he had time to glimpse Ben. The smug git did nothing to help; he stood aside with a satisfied smirk on his face as he watched Failenn and Sonya wrestle.

He dove on top of the witch, ready to haul her off Sonya, but the pair rolled over so that Sonya was on top and he was cast aside. The women flipped once more until Failenn straddled Sonya. He reached for Failenn's shoulders, but the witch evaded his grasp.

Sonya's eyes bulged, her face puce, under the weight of the witch. How strange that Failenn was a corporeal form? Why wasn't she a ghost, an ethereal presence that couldn't cause physical harm?

He already knew the answer; the energy he had given her over the past couple of months had given her strength. She had fed on his fear, becoming a solid being, more than an astral imprint. She was almost flesh and blood again, a solid mass of ectoplasm, as close to a fully reincarnated person as she could be in the present time.

But it wasn't enough for her. She wanted more. Being solid ectoplasm wasn't enough. No, she had to take over a human being, usurp their body.

"Sonya, watch out, Failenn wants to take over your body! You made yourself vulnerable to her by believing Ben's lies!"

He grabbed the witch's shoulders, but as he tried to pull, he felt arms around his chest. Ben tore him away from Failenn and he rolled across the grass.

"No, Ben, stop. Get out of my way." He scrabbled across the lawn on all fours and knocked Ben's legs from under him in his attempt to reach the fighting women. Sonya was managing on her own, but barely. She was taller than Failenn and used her long arms to bench-press the witch upwards off her body, causing the vengeful spirit to release the throttle hold on her throat. Sonya managed to get a leg in under the witch, placing her foot on Failenn's stomach, and kicked her away. The witch fell backwards, crashing against him as he stumbled to his feet. The air was knocked out of his lungs as the heavy ectoplasmic form landed on top of him. For a ghost, Failenn sure was heavy.

Stars danced in front of his eyes for several seconds as he lay winded. Failenn wasted no time and dived again for Sonya, who screamed as the witch attacked her.

"Ben, help me – please!" Sonya cried.

A knife of hurt pierced his heart. In her moment of fear and desperation, Sonya had called for Failenn's accomplice, a reincarnated soldier intent on harming them both, rather than him, her boyfriend of the past twelve years.

Ex-boyfriend.

Tears prickled the corners of his eyes and he sniffed them back. Hurt or not, he would save Sonya and show her that *he* was the real man in her life, not a malign medieval mercenary who had tricked her.

As Sonya and Failenn fought, Ben rounded on him. Ben was a couple of inches taller than him; around six foot tall, and had more muscle. Not only that, but he was faster. He tried to land a hook to the bastard's jaw, but Ben blocked it with his forearm and threw a cross at the same time. Matthew staggered backwards, blood bursting from his nose in a fountain. Heat spread across his cheeks; he hoped his nose wasn't broken, though if it was, there was nothing he could do about it at that moment. He concentrated all his energy and hurtled towards Ben, throwing an overhand punch. Ben clearly saw it a mile away, as he struck him again and again, landing blow after blow on his face and body. Every part of his body ached, and he felt helpless to stop the rain of blows, helpless to stop Failenn's relentless attack on Sonya.

The witch grabbed a shirt from the ground and wrapped it over Sonya's arms, pinning her as though in a straitjacket. She sat on Sonya's thighs, immobilising her legs. Ben turned his attention away from him and pressed down on Failenn's back, squashing her into Sonya.

Failenn's trick gave him an idea; he grabbed a shirt and looped it over Ben's head, pulling the sleeves so that the fabric tugged tightly on his throat. Ben gagged and gasped as he yanked him backwards off the women.

The bastard rolled aside, his mouth wide open for air; a pathetic fish dying, out of its element.

Sonya lay flat on her back, clutching her neck as she too gasped for air.

Failenn was gone.

Where was the witch? He looked behind to see if she had gone back into the house, but it was impossible; she had been sandwiched between Ben and Sonya and hadn't moved. Had her ghostly form disappeared into thin air, back to the spirit world, maybe? Such an idea didn't make sense; the ectoplasm forming her body had been all-too solid, carrying real weight.

Ben sat up and glared at him.

Sonya set up and fixed a menacing glare at him too. Instead of her warm, brown eyes, her gaze was cold and dazzling green.

With a shiver, he realised what had happened. The witch hadn't disappeared.

Sonya was possessed.

CHAPTER THIRTY-TWO

Easter of 1316 had arrived. Aymer thought wistfully of the new crops that wouldn't come this year. Famine, and fire had ravaged the countryside. All that was left was destruction left in a blazing trail by the Scots.

But amidst destruction, spring brought with it new hope. Two days before, on the 8th April, fifteen galleys had arrived from Drogheda; a much needed relief force. Lord Thomas De Mandeville had ordered the galleys to be arrested and pressed into service to reinforce Carraig Fhearghais Castle. They had to resist the Scots using any means possible.

Was it a bad omen that the galleys had arrived during a truce between the garrison holed up in Carraig Fhearghais and the Scottish besiegers? The Scots had not been expecting any fight; and Lord Mandeville had then attacked.

Aymer recalled the skirmish, no sooner than the reinforcements had disembarked the fifteen galleys. They had surprised the unprepared Scots, killing thirty in the skirmish and causing the rest to take flight.

Now Lord Mandeville planned to attack again. Aymer searched deep in his gut where a hollow fear lingered, and within his bones, where a chill settled. Every sense in his body told him it was the wrong move; but the Lord was in command and he had been emboldened by their success two days before.

No sooner than the thoughts had crossed his mind, Aymer heard an order issued on the still air. "Lord Mandeville calls us all. There are only sixty men under one guard by the name of Neil Fleming. The time has come to strike the Scots down, for once and for all. We are strong now that we have the reinforcements."

Could that be true; the Scots were still unprepared after an attack only two days before? Aymer listened to the call and felt the blood pump as a hot surge through his body. He dressed quickly alongside fellow soldiers in Henry Thrapston's garrison. Over the top of his gambeson and jerkin, he wore a red surcoat emblazoned with a yellow cross with the red hand of Ulster in the centre; a blood-red right hand with its palm facing forwards and fingers aligned upwards. In his right hand he carried a falchion, and in his left arm, his large wooden flat-topped shield, reinforced with leather.

The foot-soldiers moved swiftly towards the Portcullis, following Lord Mandeville.

Aymer understood. While the enemy had fled Carraig Fhearghais town to assemble more of their own forces, their own reinforced garrison could try a sally. It was a brilliant plan. Even as the notion formed in his mind, Aymer saw Lord Mandeville send a small party of messengers ahead, numbering six men who moved with stealth out of the castle, ready to alarm the Scots.

Blossom leaves fluttered as the portcullis was raised. The sound of grating metal was met by the soft whistle of wind between the twin round towers of the gatehouse.

As he passed out of the gate, Aymer looked upwards at the archers lining the machicolations, ready for the enemy if the sally didn't work.

"Surround the sixty Scots," Lord Mandeville shouted. "We will prevent their escape and slaughter them all!"

The foot-soldiers parted ways, a portion of troops veering left and the rest to the right, directed by Lord Mandeville. Aymer remained with a small, chosen body of soldiers following Lord Mandeville straight ahead through the Main Street of Carraig Fhearghais town.

Edward Bruce's banners lay ahead. He was surrounded by his royal household and, like a boulder in the pit of his stomach, Aymer saw ten Galloglasses surrounding them. The terrifying Gaelic mercenaries dwarfed the strongest foot-soldiers, head and shoulders higher than the tallest man. Behind lay two hundred spearmen, led by the knight, John Mac Nakill, rows of Scottish soldiers, ready to attack.

Not sixty men led by Neil Fleming; men numbering close to three hundred all in all, ready for war.

This was a mistake.

But he would never retreat.

They had to go, or they would lose.

No surrender!

Lord Mandeville, mounted on his half-stud stallion, raised his sword to the sky. "Now of a truth shall men see how we can die for our master!"

With a rallying cry, the foot-soldiers moved forward as one mass. Aymer moved with them, falchion in his right hand and a shield in his left.

The momentary bravado that Aymer had generated was knocked out of him as he took a cudgel to his chest. His enemy was a tall, broad man, but not as thickset as he, and dressed in the Scottish red and yellow tunic. Winded, Aymer nevertheless swung his falchion, high over his right shoulder in an arc, bringing it down towards the soldier's left temple. The man – black haired and bearded like himself – was leaner and quicker, ducking away before the falchion could find its target.

"Colbyn, that was close. Watch your back!"

The cry, by one of the Scottish soldier's fellow men at arms, alerted Aymer. Aymer and Colbyn fell apart as a knight on horseback charged between them. The knight could easily have struck him down, though he was not the target. It was Gilbert Harper, who made straight for Lord Mandeville, no doubt recognising his family crest. Aymer watched, horror-struck, as Gilbert Harper's squire threw a spear from the left, distracting Lord Mandeville. As Mandeville turned to defend himself against the squire, Harper closed in behind him. He swung his battle axe high over himself in a sweeping, circular movement across his own body, up over his left shoulder and behind his own head, then brought it round his right side. Mandeville turned to face him too late, and raised his shield too high, opening up his left arm pit. Harper's battle axe connected with the exposed hole in the gambeson, protected only by mail armour. Lord Mandeville keeled to the right, dead before he fell from his horse.

"Retreat! We need to retreat! Back to the castle."

Aymer heard the cry, amidst a flurry as both Henry Thrapston's men and Lord Mandeville's reinforcements broke for the safety of Carraig Fhearghais Castle. He followed the stampede back through the ravaged town. As they neared the portcullis, Aymer saw the bridge drawing up.

"No. No. Wait, damn you, don't leave us to the fury of these dratted victors." His curse floated unheard in the cacophony of dying men and panicked soldiers. Only one thing mattered. He had to get inside the castle. Inside to safety to fight another day.

"Why do these Scots torment us? Ulster has nothing to do with them?" His boots thundered onwards, barely touching the ground; his chest burned as air swirled in and out in a desperate rush to keep him alive.

He made it. He had reached the safety of the castle. The bridge drew up behind him, the gates were shut behind the last few men who had fled the Scots. Aymer drew a breath of relief as he let his body slow, slow and stop. He let his mind stop too; for as much as he had been spared, the fate of their men who had been left to fend for themselves outside the castle was unimaginable. It didn't bear thinking about. Victory would have to wait.

CHAPTER THIRTY-THREE

Two against one. Matthew knew he was in trouble.

Ben had him pinned, face down on the ground, with a knee on his shoulder blades. He could feel Sonya sitting on his legs and cold fingers fumbling as she tightened a belt around his wrists, tethering his arms behind his back. Sonya never had cold hands; she had a high metabolism and always tended to be on the warm side. It was the witch possessing her; Failenn in her body, making her as cold as a corpse.

The thought was terrifying. He bucked and writhed but was helpless against his captors. Medieval captors: not his ex-girlfriend and recently detached parasitic twin. Foes from the past that wanted to destroy him in the present.

They frog-marched him towards the house, causing him to stumble, Sonya in front dragging him by the collar and Ben behind, steering him by the shoulders. The garden path had become a bridge over a motte, and the house a castle. As they crossed the threshold, and the open front doorway cast them into shadow, an image of a raised portcullis looming above filtered into his mind. The enemy was entering his fortress; two medieval assailants from the opposing army. He was vulnerable, he was afraid.

"Why are you doing this? I'm ready to talk things through, like you both want." He struggled, but they had too tight a grip on him. He'd have to save his energy for the right moment.

"The time for discussion has passed," Ben answered.

"There's always time for discussion if we're being reasonable," he panted. "Come on, we're all adults."

"You're the one who threw all the clothes out the window, so don't talk about being an adult," Sonya chided.

They marched him up the stairs. With a shove on the small of his back, he found himself pushed into the spare room. He stumbled and fell on the bed; Sonya tethered his feet to the bottom of the bedframe with a bathrobe belt, while Ben overpowered him and tied his hands to the headboard using shoelaces. There was no hope of escape for him now; he was their prisoner, to do with what they would.

"What are you doing? Don't do this. Please, let's talk," he begged.

Sonya rushed out, leaving Ben to check the knots in the tethers, binding him to the bedframe. He heard her footsteps thumping downstairs and the sound of the front door opening, before she returned a few minutes later.

"Since you're going to be here until we decide otherwise, here's something to keep you occupied. Leftovers that we picked up on the way home." Her tone was mocking. He craned his neck to look at her smirking face; she stood in the doorway holding a poke of chips wrapped in a greasy newspaper, which she threw at him. The chips scattered across the bed leaving its crumpled newspaper wrapping discarded on his crotch.

Ben backed out of the room with a sneer, and Sonya with a derisive laugh, but neither saying a word. They slammed the door shut, and he strained his ears to hear them talking on the landing outside.

Ben's voice. *What are we going to do with him? We can't keep him locked up forever.*

Sonya's response. *Yes, we can. Who's going to notice?*

Ben, after a pause. *People will notice the change at work.*

Sonya. *No, they won't. You're his boss. Pretend he left. Or got fired.*

His heart hammered in his chest. Were they going to kill him? Starve him to death? Torture him, then starve him to death? "Help!" he shouted. "I'm being held prisoner, help me!"

A bang on the door, making it rattle in its frame. "Shut up, Matthew. You aren't helping yourself," said Ben.

The smell of the scattered chips filled the room. They were strewn all across his body, though none near his face. He studied the crumpled newspaper that lay on his crotch. It was a page from the *Belfast Telegraph*, a few weeks earlier, on the 10th of August. The Headline jumped out: *DUP's Sammy Wilson says Leo Varadkar has 'cheek' to come to Belfast as NI 'nothing to do with him'.*

Nothing to do with him. Those words were familiar. But from where.

Aymer? Hadn't he said something similar? The vision was already fading from his thoughts. Sonya's hushed voice, outside the spare bedroom door, distracted him further.

"We'll have to keep watch on him," said the witch, in his girlfriend's voice.

Footsteps retreating, creaks on the stairs. His captors were leaving.

A tap on the window alerted him. He rolled his head to the left and saw a seagull sitting on the window ledge.

Was it attracted by the smell of the chips? Couldn't be; the window was shut. The seagull pecked at the glass, but to no avail. It didn't matter, he supposed; the witch could still monitor him with her psionic ability from outside. So, that was what she meant by 'keep watch on him'. The seagull was there for him, not the chips. It was no different than having a security camera, or a baby monitor in the room.

Of course, a bird outside was no major threat to him. It couldn't stop him from calling for help; they certainly hadn't taped his mouth shut. Maybe they would soon, but for now he would do anything to alert the neighbours on the other side of their semi-detached house.

"Help! I'm being held hostage in the spare room."

The seagull tapped at the window with its beak.

"There are two kidnappers. Their names are Sonya and Ben."

The seagull pecked, harder.

"Call 999. Send the police!"

The seagull squawked a protest.

With horror, he watched as the window clicked open. Maybe the handle had been loose. Maybe the catch had been broken. Neither Sonya nor he used the spare room much; they hadn't checked the window.

The seagull pushed the window open with its head and hopped into the room. It sat on the inside windowsill and fixed its beady eyes on him.

He had to be rational. Despite Failenn's psionic control of the bird, it was still a real animal; an animal that she possessed. He would have to tap into its underlying animal brain, to frighten the creature physically so that it would fly away. But how, when he was tethered to the bedframe?

"Shoo," he shouted. "Go on, scat!"

The bird fluttered, then tucked its wings firmly back at its sides.

"Caw!" he yelled, in imitation of a crow.

The seagull hopped onto the foot of the bed. It pecked at a chip.

Okay, so clearly scaring the bird away wasn't working; Failenn's power over it was too strong. He needed new tactics: think. Think.

"Listen, Failenn. Whatever injustice I did to you in a past life is buried so deeply that I don't even know consciously what it was. You've shown me so many memories of that former life – but not whatever crime Aymer committed. I don't think that's fair, do you?"

The seagull hopped closer until it was sitting on his shins. The bird ate another chip.

"Maybe you're playing a game with me, trying to torture me a bit. But if your real motive is revenge, then shouldn't you at least reveal everything to me? What are Aymer's secrets?"

The bird hopped closer still and sat on his thighs.

"What did Aymer do to you? Or was it something to your dad, Beollan?"

It hopped onto his pelvis, on top of the newspaper covered in chip grease. He watched the picture of Sammy Wilson and Leo Varadkar's faces squashed under the seagull's weight.

He gulped, before continuing. "What about Colbyn? Did Aymer commit a crime against him when they were both 14ᵗʰ century soldiers?"

The seagull fixed a black, beady eye on him, cocking its head so that it looked at him from only its left side. It pecked at a chip on his stomach.

"It was war back then; they were both men at arms. Soldiers kill, that's what they do. Aymer had fair game to defend himself against a Scottish enemy who was trying to take over what was rightfully his – Carrickfergus town where he lived. Don't you agree?"

The seagull didn't make a sound. In one swift move, it pivoted forward like a dashboard bobblehead bird. The sharp beak struck him right on the incision from his operation that had only just healed. It pierced a hole, right above where his appendix was and dug its beak inside his abdomen.

Matthew threw his head back on the pillow and screamed.

CHAPTER THIRTY-FOUR

Spasms of pain crested and troughed, assaulting every nerve ending in his body. His back arched and straightened. He bucked and writhed. Buffeted, on an endless sea of pain. He was a wave on an ocean, a white-capped swell in the North channel, neither here nor there. Neither Irish, nor Scottish. Anglo-Irish. Anglerfish. A small fry, a miniscule prey in an infinite sea, moving towards the light. The sea of life. How many lifetimes?

Captive. He was trapped, drawn into a complex game that spanned eight centuries.

The seagull pecked. Matthew shrieked.

Amidst the unrelenting torture, he managed to look downwards along his body. The bird tugged and a long, silvery cord emerged from the wound in his abdomen. His intestine? The seagull pulled and a bulge appeared beneath the skin, causing a hillock in his stomach. The wound widened, the skin splitting open, and a slippery silver mass emerged, a grapefruit-sized ghostly ball. It was the ghost of his parasitic twin brother before his transformation into Ben. The ghost foetus-in-foetu pointed its tentacle at him, like a fleshy root on a grotesque human tree. The skin puckered once, then twice at two points not three inches apart and two eyelids appeared. They fluttered open. Two eyes appeared beneath, watching him. The silvery eyelids blinked a few times, but the piercing eyes, not unlike his own, never moved their gaze from him.

"Argh!"

He screamed until his throat was hoarse. For being a ghost, it sure felt real, a heavy ectoplasmic form as the witch, Failenn, had been before she was absorbed inside Sonya's body. He arched his abdomen upwards in a feeble attempt to buck the mutated monstrosity off but couldn't. The foetus-in-foetu responded by sprouting more tentacles until it had four grotesque rudimentary limbs grasping at him. The leg tentacles circled around each thigh, gripping the fabric of his trousers and the arm tentacles slithered upwards over his abdomen, towards his face.

"No. Get off. What do you want from me?"

The seagull hopped off him and sat alongside them on the bed. It flapped its wings with excitement as it goaded his parasitic twin on its slow journey towards his face.

"You're a tumour, you're a parasite, and I gave you life! I had you removed, and now you're better than ever as Ben. You should be thanking me, not torturing me."

The parasitic twin inched forward with soft squelching sounds as the tentacles pushed and pulled it over his chest.

"How can you even be a ghost if you're downstairs? You turned into Ben. How is this possible?" he gasped.

"I am the ghost of what has passed," said the foetus-in-foetu. "And what must be rectified in the present."

"No, wait! Be reasonable. Why are you doing this? Show me what I've done wrong. Let me at least know the full story."

The last time he had seen the fleshy mass, it had been in a past vision: of Aymer hanged on the gallows, cut open in the middle of medieval Béal Feirste. That vision alone had not been chronological, like the others he had witnessed, which had shown a succinct tale of a Scottish foe attacking the Anglo-Irish garrison at Carrickfergus Castle.

"The last time I saw you, Failenn lifted you out of Aymer's dead body back in 1316, or something, in medieval Béal Feirste. I saw all of the other visions of Aymer through his eyes – except that one. Why did the witch show me that one?"

"Failenn wanted you to see Aymer's fate," said the ghostly parasitic twin.

"Aymer didn't have a parasitic twin, though, like I did. So, why were you there?"

The foetus-in-foetu grinned, but said nothing.

"You – and the witch – were ghosts during that vision of Aymer at the gallows. You were able to appear because of a connection. A channel between past and present."

The fabric of time ripping open, like loose threads unravelling, to create a hole.

A hole in his gut, where a parasitic brother had been removed.

"You took my life in the past and you are trying to take my life now," said his twin.

"I nurtured you for thirty-three years, in my body. I gave you life. But you're trying to take mine. By stealing my house and my job and my woman, you're trying to take mine!"

"You have no idea. None. About anything," said his brother. The tentacle-arms slithered up over his throat.

"Then show me," he pleaded.

They crept up over his chin.

"Veniam ad vos," the ghostly fleshy mass said.

He translated the Latin in his head: I am coming for you.

The tentacles snaked over his lips. He felt one enter his right nostril and the other enter his left nostril.

"Argh! Get off me, what are you doing?"

But he already knew the answer. It was going to connect with his brain, show him what he needed to see.

Intense pressure started in the bridge of his nose. The tentacles moved deeper inside his head and a flash of light filled both eyes, along with searing pain as though a bolt of lightning had struck him in the face. He sensed his parasitic twin stimulating his optic nerve; it was as though a video camera had been switched on, overtaking his vision.

He saw a crowd of people dressed in medieval peasant clothing: linen tunic shirts, heavily patched, cropped woollen trousers, most without shoes, their soles toughened from a hard life. They carried sticks, rocks, anything that could be used as missiles. They were running through heather, swiping brambles in their path. He heard angry voices carrying across the still night air.

"Catch the traitor," a man shouted. Matthew's mind translated the Gaelic into modern English by way of instinct. He had known Gaelic once, in a former life.

He understood. The townspeople of early fourteenth century Carraig Fhearghais were chasing Failenn's father, Beollan, upwards towards the top of Beann Mhadagáin's Peak outside the small village of Béal Feirste.

It was Failenn's memory, shown by psionic connection through the ghost of his parasitic twin. A ghost that had been unleashed by the witch's servant: her seagull.

The memory, forced as a cinema reel along his optic nerve, continued.

The townspeople caught up with Beollan. His heart raced. He knew what was coming.

His eyes rested on the boy who had caught Failenn's father. The boy was around fourteen or fifteen, not yet at his full adult height, still lean and wiry, but already broad in the shoulders. His sinewy legs had caught up to the older man with ease; his broad shoulders had provided the power to hold Beollan until the other men reached him and bound him to a makeshift pyre.

Failenn had shown him this vision before. Orange and yellow flames consumed her father, Beollan. But this time, his attention turned to the teenage boy.

Who was the adolescent, on the verge of becoming a man, with the makings of a great future man-at-arms?

Aymer. It was his former incarnation when he had existed seven hundred years before.

Aymer had been the first captor to lay hands on Beollan, allowing the stronger men among the Carraig Fhearghais townspeople to bring Failenn's father to vigilante justice. It was Aymer's fault that Beollan hadn't escaped his fate.

CHAPTER THIRTY-FIVE

The information was a revelation. Aymer – Matthew in a former life – had been culpable for Beollan's death, and hence the witch's revenge.

The knowledge was such a painful realisation that it shot, like a bolt of lightning, from his brain, through his nose, down the tentacle-arm of the ghost foetus-in-foetu and straight into the seagull that was perched on his hips. Like an electric shock, the bird hopped into the air with a squawk.

In a flash of light, he saw himself lying tethered on the bed. Comprehension dawned; his consciousness had travelled into the bird. He had acquired Failenn's psionic ability.

Matthew-seagull flapped his wings and took to the air. He flopped back down in a clumsy mess of feathers. The transition from man to bird had been so fast, his new body needed a few minutes to coordinate itself. After a moment's focus, he channelled his animal-brain and directed the instructions from his mind to his powerful wings. Much smoother this time, he flew out the spare bedroom window.

The kitchen window was open by a few inches. Not enough to get inside the house, but enough to eavesdrop at a safe distance. He swooped downwards and perched on the concrete ledge outside.

Inside, Ben poured himself another cup of coffee. His eyes rolled upwards to the left as though listening for any sound in the spare bedroom above.

"It's all gone silent. Do you think he burned himself out trying to escape?" said Ben.

Sonya, her back to him as she set her coffee mug in the sink, shook her head. "No. He saw what he wanted to see. He knows the truth about his part in my father's death."

"You mean, Failenn's father's death?"

She spun around, her green eyes full of the devil's fire. "I *am* Failenn, and don't you ever doubt that again. Didn't I tell you I would get revenge? Didn't I assure you of your victory over him?"

"You assured me of the Scottish victory and that my own glory would take longer. Glory over what? Matthew — Aymer — lives. He mocked me at Carrickfergus Castle, he mocked me into submission for thirty-three years inside his body and now what? I've waited a very long time."

Her face broke into a teasing grimace. "Then you can wait a bit longer. He has more to learn, and I have more punishment to inflict on him."

"Believe me, I want Aymer-Matthew to suffer too. For the atrocities he committed, for the injustice he inflicted upon Beollan, and upon you, and upon me. But I have waited for seven hundred years. When will justice be served?"

"Soon. What do we say to the enemy? Veniam ad vos," she crooned.

Matthew clicked his beak. Sonya was possessed by the witch; she wasn't responsible for her evil part in tying him up in the spare room. But Ben was another matter. Ben had denied that he was one and the same as the menacing medieval mercenary, Colbyn, who wanted to destroy him in vengeance against Aymer. Matthew clicked his beak again in outrage. Once his consciousness was out of the seagull, and if he ever escaped from his tethers on the bedframe upstairs, he would pummel Ben to a pulp, brother of his, or not.

As though guided by an unseen connection, Ben strode to the kitchen window and peered out the gap. His eyes set immediately on the seagull. Matthew flapped and hopped down onto the grass.

"Failenn, get over here. Isn't that the bird you had set to watching Matthew upstairs?" Ben jabbed an accusing finger at Matthew-seagull and he ruffled his feathers, ready to take flight.

Sonya joined him at the window, turning her possessed green eyes of the witch towards him. "Yes. Why isn't it watching him? If I set my inner eye to a task, it goes where I direct it, guided by the Graceful Goddess of the Lunar Light."

"Maybe our talking distracted your concentration on the bird and its mind was released?" Ben suggested.

She scratched her nose in thought. "No, that wouldn't have severed my psionic connection. Come to think of it, I haven't sensed Matthew through the bird for about ten minutes, at least."

Ben and Sonya looked at each other.

"You don't think he could be dead, do you?" said Ben.

As both of them turned for the door, Matthew-seagull took flight. He had to get back into his body before they got to it first.

CHAPTER THIRTY-SIX

When the bridge had been drawn up, and the portcullis lowered, Aymer knew that had been the beginning of the end for their garrison, holed up as they were in Carraig Fhearghais Castle with little provisions left. They had struggled on for two months after the relief force from Drogheda had arrived. To say that Lord Mandeville's defeat had been dispiriting for the men was a gross understatement. The remaining men in Mandeville's and Henry Thrapston's combined forces were beyond devastation; they knew the writing was on the wall.

June 1316. The midsummer sun seemed to taunt them in their isolation and starvation. They drew water from the well running through the entry floor of the Keep, but little else. The hides they had been reduced to chewing had long since been consumed. As provisions waned, so did any chatter inside the walls of the keep. A still, ominous air hung over the castle, and a strong sense of doom lingered, with a stench of death.

Death. Words of death, carried in a soft croon, breaking the silence of the summer air.

"The famine has seen all crops fail
and young and old alike do wail
as men eat their own fallen horses,
and graveyards serve up meals of corpses,
bodies in hunger, minds full of fear,
death is coming very near,
as women cook and eat their young,
their pitiful lives so short, forever unsung."

The taunting lyrics were delivered by a woman's voice, floating soft as a maiden's, but with an edge as that of one who had lived a hardened life. Aymer didn't recognise the voice, but he knew from the delivery of her words that she was local, not one of the Scottish foe.

He had heard rumours, unsubstantiated, but rife within the castle, that the woman's words were true. The Annals of Dubh Linn had talked of many feeding on horse flesh, and some reports had even suggested that dead bodies had been roasted by those starved of corn, crop and lea. Maybe that was what made her words so ominous. Aymer shuddered, the chill exacerbated by the gnawing hunger in his empty gut, the weight of the singer's words bearing down on him, heavy in his starving bowels.

"It is over. We are to surrender."

He heard the words floating down from above; one among the machicolations. The stone walls of his own fortress crumbled around him. Surrender. It was all over. He crumpled to his knees, then sank onto his haunches, letting his body succumb to defeat. Physically, emotionally, intellectually. Life as he knew it was over.

"Thirty of the Scots are to enter. They have won. They are going to seize control. We are to give into their terms if we are to be spared."

Spared didn't exist. Spared meant death. It was a veiled threat from the enemy.

In spite of how his body sank to the ground, like spilled groats from a moth-eaten sack, Aymer found his jaw hardening and his will resolving, in defiance of the reality around him. The situation in the castle was untenable, yet one mantra flooded him:

No surrender.

He pulled himself to his feet, clawing his way upright using another's hauberk for grip.

"No," he gasped. "No surrender. We can't be defeated. We must fight to the bitter end."

"This is the bitter end, Aymer. We are done," said his fellow man-at-arms.

He shook his head, tossing it to and fro in defiance of the wind, of the woman singer, of the Scottish enemy.

"No, damn you. We fight."

The gaunt face of his companion furrowed in despair. "How do you propose we do that? With what strength?"

"Thirty of the enemy are coming within our walls. Let's not be overtaken. Let us not allow them to set our terms," he cried.

"He's right," said another soldier. "What do you say, Aymer?"

"We invite them in, under agreement that we will submit to their rule," he started.

The men watched him.

"We raise the portcullis, letting them think they have won," he went on.

The men waited.

"Then we seize them and take them as prisoners," he finished, with a satisfied smile.

"Yes, let's throw them in the Gatehouse. It's the best guarded place," added another.

"No." His voice was unwavering, in spite of his hunger-weakened body. "It has to be the small towers of the Middle Ward. We'll thrown them in the oubliette. There will be no escaping from that."

CHAPTER THIRTY-SEVEN

"Matthew? Are you alive?"

Sonya turned away from him, tethered to the bedframe, to Ben, standing next to her at the open spare room door.

His consciousness had jolted back into his body moments before they had entered the room; wings were faster than legs. But he was as good as dead, his body numb, as though soul and flesh weren't quite attached. It was lucky timing; maybe if they thought he was dead, that would buy him time to come up with a plan for how to fight such powerful entities.

Ben's eyes studied his body; every inch from his head to his feet. His head had lolled to the right side, his mouth slack and eyes open, but for all Ben and Sonya knew, unseeing. He could feel perspiration on his brow and the dampness under his armpits and across his chest. Looking down his own body, he could see his hands were the colour of porridge, a giveaway that he was close to death. Ben's eyes travelled lower to the gaping hole in his abdomen and he saw that the stitches from his surgery had been ripped open, the edges red and inflamed. Green pus had leaked out across his midriff. It took a moment to register what he was seeing; of course there was a hole, the seagull had ripped it when it allowed the ghost of his parasitic twin to escape and taunt him.

"He must be dead. Doesn't seem like he's breathing," Ben said. "The wound is open."

Sonya glared at him; he could feel the witch's eyes boring the hole in him even wider.

"He can't be dead. I wasn't finished with him."

"Why don't you check his pulse?" Ben jerked his thumb in his direction. What a rude bastard; not even a respectful gesture, and for all his foe knew, he was standing over a corpse.

Sonya scowled. "Why should I? I don't want to touch him. Filthy murderer."

Ben's face crumpled in dismay. "I wanted him to suffer more too. But we have to know for sure, before we dispose of the body."

Matthew concentrated his thoughts; maybe, if he could appeal to Sonya's consciousness, hidden deep within the witch's possession of her, then she might fight Failenn and help rescue him.

Help me, Sonya. Untie me! Fight the witch, and Ben too. Fight!

She crossed the room to the right side of the bed and crouched down by his face. Had she heard his appeal? She placed a hand on his neck. "I can't feel a pulse."

He tried to talk, but his tongue lay benign in his mouth. Cold numbness still filled every part of him.

Ben looked thoughtful. "How are we going to dispose of the body?"

"We'll take him up onto Beann Mhadagáin's Peak and burn him. Give him the punishment that he inflicted upon my father," said the witch, in Sonya's voice.

Ben's face was pale. "Béal Feirste is different than it was. We can't transport a body without being seen. We'll have to find another way."

Sonya's brow creased, as the witch thought hard. "Why don't we call his parents first, say he was ill from an infection in his wound? They can find the body. There's nothing untoward with the corpse that would suggest otherwise."

"If we're going to do that, we should at least untie him first as that'll look bad on us," Ben added.

A wicked grin came over Sonya's face. "We can say he went up to rest and we found him like this. And we'll say the reason you're here is that you were worried about him because he hadn't shown up at work, so you thought you'd stop by and check up on him."

Ben grinned in agreement with the witch. "Okay, that sounds like a good plan. That makes sense."

Matthew studied Ben. There was no point appealing to the spirit of his brother, buried in the unconscious mind of resurrected Colbyn. He would have to try again to contact Sonya, using his psionic ability.

Fight, Sonya. You and I together could win over Colbyn and Failenn. Fight!

If his message had reached Sonya, beyond Failenn's possession of her, he had no way to know; she gave no indication that she understood, at all.

Burning pain started in his gut and spread outwards, like a ripple on a pond. On the one hand, he was glad that feeling had returned to his body as soon he would have the strength to shout for help, and to fight to his death, if need be. But for now, the agony consumed him. Cold sweat broke out all over his body. He felt clammy and uncomfortable, his neck slick as salt water trickled across his face, pooling behind his head.

To his dismay, Sonya turned her back and walked towards the door.

No, don't leave! Help me, Sonya.

Once again, the thoughts didn't leave his head. Ben turned to follow her out, but before he left, he cast a faint smile back at Matthew's deathbed. Dismay turned to horror as he realised that his parents, his innocent, trusting parents – were going to be in danger very soon.

Sonya, fight! Don't let the witch bring my parents here. I'm not dead – help me fight. Kick her out of your body, Sonya, you have to!

No use! His words couldn't be transmitted beyond thought; the witch was too strong, blocking him.

So be it. He would have to take his metaphysical fight elsewhere. He would channel his psionic ability and use it to take action where the problems had started in the first place.

In the past.

CHAPTER THIRTY-EIGHT

By closing his eyes, Matthew allowed his consciousness to sink into comforting depths. A greyish twilight surrounded him, and a faint light in the distance. He must have been floating, for he couldn't feel himself walking. The pinpoint of light ahead became a band across the horizon and as he approached, it engulfed him.

He blinked as his eyes adjusted to the brightness. The shag carpet beneath his feet was made of thick, mustard-coloured wool. The wallpaper was striped; salmon pink and duck-egg blue. He recognised the garish décor; it was his childhood living room.

A small boy, around four years old, sat on the carpet. The boy's dark hair was cut in a pudding bowl style, and he played on the carpet with a *Fireman Sam* set of toys.

"I remember those toys," he said.

He looked closer at the boy, and as he studied his face, the child looked up at him and they locked eyes momentarily.

It was himself as a nursery school-age kid.

Child-Matthew turned away from present-Matthew and looked towards the living room door. Another boy appeared in the open doorway. He had a hazy outline, as he stood in the sunlight flooding the living room. Like child-Matthew, the boy was dark-haired with similar large, brown doe-eyes. The child crossed the room and crouched down opposite child-Matthew on the shag carpet. He picked up the *Fireman Sam* fire engine and began vrooming it across the bumpy carpet.

"I wasn't finished with that," said child-Matthew, in his squeaky, preschool voice. "Give it back."

"You had it long enough," said the other boy, a distinct echo to his voice.

Present-Matthew stuck a finger in his ear and wiggled it around. Could the echo be because he was watching a memory? Clearly this was a moment that he had locked up in his brain and was now recalling from the depths of his subconscious. If so, physically poking his ear wouldn't help matters. Though, why child-Matthew didn't also have an echo to his voice was a mystery.

"But they're my toys," child-Matthew protested.

"No, they're mine," the other boy argued, his voice resonating with a ghostly echo.

The other boy snatched the *Fireman Sam* figure out of child-Matthew's hand.

"Mu-um! Elmer isn't playing fair! He's not sharing!"

Elmer. A coldness sank through present-Matthew's core, like he had swallowed an ice-cube whole. He studied the second boy, and a horrible reality began to dawn on him. The child, crouched opposite his childhood self, continued to be outlined by the hazy grey aura that had surrounded him when he stood in the sunlight of the living room door moments before. But there, on the floor, where the sunlight didn't reach, he still glowed with a greyish outline.

Elmer was his childhood imaginary friend.

A ghost. A figment of his imagination.

Present-Matthew gulped. He had repressed the memories; forgotten the imaginary boy he had once played with twenty-eight years ago.

"Elmer, so it's you. You were always there. I was Aymer in a former life, so I named you after myself – the modern-day variant of my past-life name. You were the ghost of Colbyn, that Scottish soldier in the thirteen hundreds. I named you Elmer because I wanted to make you my friend. My brother."

The ghostly Elmer looked up at present-Matthew and instead of the doe-eyed gaze, a deadness lingered in those dark eyes, a hollowness that absorbed all light in the room, not reflected it. He shivered.

"You lived inside me, inside the parasitic mass that grew in my body."

Elmer continued his shark-eyed stare.

"I was able to talk to you, in the moments when you left my twin's body, like an out-of-body experience. We played together for many years. But I lost the ability to see you as I grew up."

Elmer said nothing. He didn't blink; only stared. "It didn't mean you went away though. You were always there, for thirty-three years inside me. Our fates always were, and always will be, intertwined."

CHAPTER THIRTY-NINE

Matthew blinked to reorientate himself. He was back in the present, tied up in his spare room, his childhood living room once again relegated to past memories.

Had he really been transported to the past, or had the memory seemed so real because it had once happened? Either way, he had unlocked important information.

Elmer. The soul of his parasitic twin brother had been able to come out of his body, at times when the fleshy mass had been asleep inside him and had transmuted into the ghostly form of a boy. His ghostly twin brother had been able to play with him as an imaginary friend, all those years ago. He thought of Ben downstairs. Through a combination of accelerated stem cell growth, combined with Failenn's witchcraft, Ben had grown from a living foetus-in-foetu, extracted from his abdomen, to a fully formed adult human in mere weeks.

It defied belief, and as a staunch sceptic, he wouldn't have believed it himself had he not witnessed all that he had in the past six weeks.

The soul that had resided inside him, that had manifested as Elmer, had been relatively benign while his parasitic twin had been inside him. But at the 'birth' of Ben only weeks before, the dormant past life of Colbyn had 'activated' harbouring all the old grudges, evil energy, and desire for revenge from seven hundred and eight years before.

What had he unleashed?

Yet, if the foetus-in-foetu had stayed within him, it would eventually have killed him. In the month prior to surgery, the pain had been unbearable.

Speaking of the foetus-in-foetu, where had the ghost of the wretched silvery monstrosity gone? Clearly it had been responsible for his newfound psionic ability; of being able to see through the seagull's eyes without Failenn's interference, but where was it now? Had it disappeared back into the ether?

As though in answer to his question, a bump from under the bed rocked the frame, jostling him on the mattress. His stomach lurched as he saw a man crawl out from underneath and stand up, facing him at the foot of the bed.

Aymer.

He looked as solid and real as he had in visions of the past, only this time he was outlined by a silvery haze, as though he was more ethereal than corporeal. Without his helmet, padded coif or mail armour, Matthew saw his past life self's features more easily than before. Aymer had long, lank brown hair and wore a dirty, beige peasant tunic. He looked somewhat emaciated. Was that due to famine and starvation as he had been holed up inside Carrickfergus Castle while the Scots surrounded it?

"If you are me, and I'm seeing you as a ghost standing in front of me, then does that mean I am only half conscious?" He nodded, answering his own question. "It does. You normally exist inside of me, as I'm your flesh reincarnation. So, if you are out of my body, then that means I'm half in the spirit world."

The apparition didn't answer. It stood, staring at him, with a neutral expression as if it didn't really see him; or register that he was there.

A sudden wave of anger beset him. "Well, say something? What is it you want? Do you realise that I am paying the price for your crimes. I didn't do anything wrong, but I'm suffering for what you did to Failenn's father, Beollan. But there's more, isn't there?"

Aymer continued to stand still, saying nothing.

"Why don't you let me know what you did, you coward!" he shouted.

Instead of speaking, Aymer gasped and spluttered as blood ran from his mouth. Ghost Aymer's abdomen split open as though unseen forces disembowelled him, spilling blood, intestines and other viscera down his legs. Rather than coating the room red with a grisly layer of blood and innards, the gore changed into twinkling specs, like dust reflecting the light in the room.

A strangled scream rattled out of Matthew's throat. He understood; he was seeing Aymer's death again. He thought back to the day, a few weeks ago, when he had first met Ben on his illicit date with Sonya. That day, he had left Robinsons pub in tears. The first meeting, in the flesh, of his parasitic twin had triggered the memory of his own demise – as Aymer – in medieval Béal Feirste, when he had hurried through the same location in modern day Cornmarket in Belfast. That ghastly vision of Aymer being hanged and disembowelled on the gallows had really happened. It was a gruesome part of Matthew's past, and inevitable present.

Death. And rebirth.

The ghost of Aymer stood before him, as a ghoulish imprint of a barbarous past. Dark shadows, like half-moons, appeared under his past-self's eyes. His skin became yellowish, the flesh of his face sunken, pooling into the hollows of his cheekbones. Aymer was wasting away before his eyes. As he changed, he resembled more of a skeleton covered with yellow wax than a muscular, fourteenth century soldier in his prime. Pockmarks began to appear on his face, giving his skin an edam-cheese complexion. The holes widened, joining to become vertical gouges. He could see the tendons underneath Aymer's rotting skin. The soldier's lips curled back exposing two rows of yellowish teeth, giving his exposed skull a death-like grimace.

The ghost-corpse continued to stand upright, decomposing as though he watched it happening in a film that was being played at ten times the speed. The flesh changed from grey to black, dropping off the bones. Greenish-grey bodily fluids oozed out of the decaying torso, dripping onto the wooden floor.

He wanted to look away, but his head was locked in place, his eyes fixed on the morbid sight, unable to shut his eyelids. Once all the flesh had rotted away, and only yellowish bones remained, the skeleton began to disintegrate. It collapsed into a mound of black mush. He studied the remains and noticed a silvery residue forming around the edges of the pile. The black mush disintegrated further until only a silvery puddle remained, as though a mugful of liquid mercury had been spilled on the floor where ghost-Aymer had stood moments before.

The silvery puddle began to rise upwards into a small dome. It grew and stretched until it became the size and form of a person with a ruddy complexion and grey hair. A man's features began to assemble, middle-aged and shorter than Aymer by about two inches at around five foot eight and far stouter than the emaciated soldier, with a protruding paunch.

Beollan. Failenn's father appeared as he had been before he had been murdered by the Carrickfergus townsfolk.

He braced himself for the inevitable; Beollan's death. "I've already seen your death – why do you torture me by showing it again? Stop, Failenn. Or if this is the ghost of my parasitic twin doing this, then I beg you, don't do this."

A flash of light shot upwards as flames consumed Beollan. Matthew let out a choked cry as the body charred black and became burned as charcoal; a shrivelled husk, resembling an effigy of a person rather than a human being. The corpse crumbled into a shower of ash and from the sooty pile, the silvery residue flowed into a larger puddle spreading outwards.

He understood. This wasn't merely about showing how figures from the past had been killed; it was about leaving an imprint, a piece of each soul joining with the ones before it to form a larger ghostly residue. The silvery substance was ectoplasm, the material from which ghosts were formed. As each past figure bled some of its psychic energy into a silvery, ectoplasmic puddle, ethereal changed to corporeal and the supernatural residue became stronger.

He could almost feel the astral energy pulsating from the silvery pool, radiating into the room. It was neither good nor evil, simply strong.

But what would strong become, if it had the power to be either? He had no time to think as another past-life incarnation began to materialise from the silvery puddle, now with as much fluid as if a kettle had been emptied of its contents.

A dull, throbbing pain spread above the bridge of his nose as he watched the next figure grow and stretch. He breathed in through his nose, out through his mouth, steadying the well of sickness in his gut and the incessant hammering of his heart as Failenn's form appeared. Her green eyes bored into him with an intensity that reflected seven centuries of hatred, her lip curled in a vengeance that she carried from beyond the grave. Her physical beauty didn't last; pockmarks began to appear all over her face and body, splitting the skin into angry red welts from which blood oozed, trickling red before coagulating into viscous, black streaks. The pockmarks varied in size, some the size of a fist, others as small as a pebble. Failenn's creamy skin began to rot, turning grey, then green as the flesh peeled from her bones. Had she been pummelled to death in her lifetime? He didn't know because she didn't want to show him – yet. Corpse-Failenn's sneering smile lingered on her decomposing face, taunting him with the knowledge that he knew nothing – yet. Her death-grimace was the last thing to fade, sliding down her face, as her flesh melted off her skull, and her skull became mush.

Failenn's rotting body disintegrated into a gelatinous ooze of bone, muscle and bodily juices; he was only thankful that he couldn't smell the decomposition, which would have added to his torture in witnessing her disgusting demise. A silvery trickle spread outwards from the corpse-puddle, making the ectoplasmic pool on the floor widen, now with as much residue as though a bucket of liquid mercury had been kicked over.

A searing pain cut through from the nape of his neck to the middle of his forehead, as though an invisible spear had been driven through his head, skewering his skull. He shrieked and thrashed on the bed, but the images wouldn't abate.

Better brace himself for the next regeneration and death; he swallowed a dry lump in his throat. It wasn't long before one more figure began to rise from the ectoplasmic pool, and Colbyn's form took shape.

Unlike in all the past-life visions of medieval Colbyn; tall, muscular and strong as a warrior in his prime should be, this version of Colbyn already looked withered. He wore a tattered tunic and Matthew saw his bony frame through holes in the fabric; had Colbyn been starved before his death in medieval Carrickfergus? Maybe the famine of the thirteen hundreds had caught up to him, as it had the rest of the country? If Colbyn was about to decompose before his eyes, he was sure it would happen quickly, as there wasn't much of him left to rot in the first place.

He fully expected that Colbyn would slowly decay as Failenn's corpse, and Aymer's had; instead, a wretched scream rattled out of his parched throat at the sudden dismemberment of his foe. Colbyn's head separated from his shoulders as an invisible sword, or axe, had lopped it off. It fell to the floor and rolled, a foot away from his bare feet. Next, his arms were hacked off. Blood spurted out from the torso, staining the rest of the body bright red. Lastly, his legs were severed near the groin, then his trunk chopped into quarters. Matthew screamed until his voice was hoarse, until his throat burned with the strain.

Unlike before when the other ghost-corpses had decayed into brown mush, there was no decomposition with Colbyn. The dismembered parts disappeared as though flesh had been scooped away in chunks. Where had the flesh gone? Left to scavengers, as in a modern-day Tibetan sky burial? Even the bones dissolved, marrow seeping out as though they had been deliberately turned to liquefaction.

Strange. Very strange.

The familiar, silvery ectoplasm spread outwards from the remains and joined the astral pool now stretching five feet across the floor, as though a barrel had been tipped over.

Through his visions of the past, he had seen Aymer's death by disembowelment and Beollan's murder by immolation in Béal Feirste; but he hadn't yet seen the manner of Failenn and Colbyn's deaths in Carraig Fhearghais. What had caused the strange pockmarks and welts on Failenn's body, and the chunks gouged out of Colbyn's corpse? If the witch was responsible for showing him the grisly scenes, then she seemed to be prolonging his torture; he knew Aymer's role in Beollan's murder, but not how he had been involved in the deaths of either medieval Failenn, or the Scottish soldier. He had a feeling the witch was going to show him soon. In a way, such a thought was a release. His pain and torment – physical, emotional, and psychological – couldn't be any worse. Failenn had reached the zenith of her powers in torturing him. Any further, and he would go beyond the bounds of what he could suffer, in this, or any other lifetime on earth.

CHAPTER FORTY

"We have caught her. We have got the singer. She's a traitor."

The woman was certainly bold. Even in irons, she continued to sing her taunting verse at the garrison.

> *"The famine has seen all crops fail*
> *and young and old alike do wail*
> *as men eat their own fallen horses,*
> *and graveyards serve up meals of corpses,*
> *bodies in hunger, minds full of fear,*
> *death is coming very near,*
> *as women cook and eat their young,*

their pitiful lives so short, forever unsung."

"She's a traitor, she's a spy for the enemy. She's been helping the Scots."

Aymer studied the face of the wench. She was not yet old; in her thirtieth summer of life, at most. She had long brown hair, which was matted and dirty from the hardship they had all felt in the past year. Her green eyes were still bright; famine hadn't yet dulled the energy in them.

A sharp, cold pain sliced through his head from the nape of his neck to the middle of his forehead, between his eyebrows. Bright light obscured any vision he had, making him blink until, gradually, his sight returned. He rested his eyes on the woman and a name came to mind: Failenn.

"Failenn!" He pointed a wavering finger at the woman. "What sorcery is this that I know her name? I haven't met this woman before, ever."

"Think again," she said, her lip curling. "We have met. A portal has opened in your mind. Use it."

He gawped at her. "Portal? What do you mean?"

"I saw the pain in your face just now, and I saw the halo of light come out of your crown, silver as the storm clouds that come for you soon."

How did the woman know about the pain? He was a seasoned soldier; he hadn't cried out with the pain. It was as though an invisible spear had pierced his head from back to front, the pain intense.

He kept a shaky finger directed at her. "What did you do to me, witch? If there is a portal, you caused it. You put it there when you inserted your name into my mind. What have I done to you? I am not your enemy. We are on the same side!"

"We are on the same side, but I am your enemy. You *do* know me. Don't you remember? I was only in my eighth summer of life, and you must have been in the sixteenth summer of yours," she spat.

As Aymer looked at her, he recalled her as a child; well-dressed, not in tatters as she stood before him now. With a gasp, he dropped his accusatory finger.

"You are Beollan's daughter. He was the Keeper of grain. He was sending grain to Carlisle – and Dumfries, and Ayr and Cockermath – while we were starving here. Your father let our own people die of hunger, while your family grew fat from food – and fat from riches from England!"

Her face curled into a sneer. "He was doing his job, no more no less. And how did you repay him? You captured him and burned him – you! All of you filthy heathens burned him. But you alone captured him. You have the most blood on your hands. I call upon the Graceful Goddess to see that you are punished!"

He looked around at the soldiers who held Failenn in irons; at the other bystanders in the courtyard who watched. "You heard her words, she is a witch."

The chains dangling from her wrists clinked as she raised her arms to the sky.

"Graceful Goddess by the Lunar Light,
Right these wrongs served in the dark night,
Beollan's death, an insult to thee,
For Aymer's crime – avenge me,
Drive this garrison from our ravaged lands,
Make them all pay; they're in your hands,
Give the castle to the Scots, let them win,
Banish the townsfolk for their crime against Sin."

"Sin? You dare speak of sin from the good word of the bible, yet you beseech a pagan goddess to punish us. It's blasphemy," he shouted.

"Sin, God of the Moon, father of our Graceful Goddess of the Lunar Light. There are no other gods, only Sin and his daughter. Know this, you heathen!" she cried, spit flying from her mouth.

"She's a witch, we must kill her before her curse on us all comes true," he said, desperation in his voice.

A dull throbbing pain centred in the front of his forehead flooded his mind with new knowledge. A name: Matthew.

"Matthew," he rasped.

"Matthew? Jesus' disciple, from the good book?" said another soldier nearby.

"It must be – the name is clear in my mind, but nothing else." He gulped. Like Failenn, he turned to the sky, but not to beseech her pagan lunar god or goddess. "Heavenly Father – send me the message from the disciple of your son, Christ."

No message entered his head, even though he concentrated hard; even though he closed his eyes to receive the information. Instead, he focused on the name Matthew.

"I was wrong. It isn't biblical Matthew. It is a man, like me. But he wants to help me. I can't hear him. But I can feel him."

CHAPTER FORTY-ONE

"Oh my God!" Matthew's heart hammered in his chest, reminding him that he was conscious, in the present, no longer surrounded by phantasms surfacing in the spare room, or trapped in another nightmarish vision from medieval Carrickfergus.

"Aymer knows who I am. Aymer in the past was able to feel my presence."

If Aymer in the past could sense him, then that meant only one thing; his newfound psionic ability was able to create a channel to communicate with his former self in the *past*.

Matthew felt his heart skip a beat: what if he could change the past? What if he could stop Aymer from killing Colbyn, or Failenn? All three of them were still alive in the most recent vision; Failenn had been captured by the garrison at Carrickfergus, but not yet killed.

What if he could change the fate of all three of them?

He hadn't yet seen either Failenn or Colbyn's deaths in the grim, medieval past which they all shared, but he knew Aymer must have had a role to play in both of their untimely ends. There was nothing he could do about Beollan's death, since the visions had been following chronologically, with the exception of his own hanging and disembowelment at the gallows, that had been triggered by the 'birth' of Ben, his parasitic twin. At the point in the sequence of events he had seen in the past, Beollan had been dead for at least twenty years; he couldn't save Failenn's father, but he could save her and Colbyn.

Would that be enough to lessen the witch's wrath against him? Failenn harboured a grudge filled with such malevolence at Aymer for her father's death; hatred and malice that had putrefied over the course of seven hundred years, bleeding into his new life on earth. He wasn't sure that saving Failenn and Colbyn could atone for his past-life crime.

There was nothing he could do about Beollan, but what stopped him from trying to change the fates of Failenn and Colbyn? He had to try. He closed his eyes and visualised Aymer's face, as a starting point. He concentrated every cell in his body, every atom of life that his living body had, into channelling the connection with Aymer.

Aymer. Can you hear me?

An answer. *Yes. Matthew? Are you a mortal man, or a disciple of God.*

His turn. *I'm a man, but I'm from a different time.*

Aymer's response: *Are you Scottish? Are you one of the enemy?*

No. He focused on the connection in his mind. *I am Northern Irish – a mix of Irish and Scottish. I live in the year two thousand and twenty-three.*

Two thousand! Aymer's response came quickly, his voice excited. He visualised his past self's surprised face.

They were getting distracted. *Aymer, listen, the witch Failenn – she is inside the castle.*

So, she is a witch! I suspected as much, and I was right. Yes, we have captured her. She will be executed as a traitor.

He shook his head, before remembering that Aymer couldn't see him, only hear his omnipotent voice. *No. Let her go. Don't put her to death.*

But we must. She helped the Scots. The writing is on the wall for us now, the castle is surrounded. Our garrison are starving. The war is lost.

This was getting tricky. *No, please, I beg you – for the sake of your immortal soul. Let her go. One life will not change the course of history – you're right that Edward Bruce has won. But you can change your fate – our destiny. Yours and mine.*

Aymer's face, that he saw in his mind, frowned. *Yours and mine? Who are you to me?*

I am you in a different time, reborn.

A pause followed. Not good; they would lose the connection if he couldn't convince Aymer soon. *Aymer, are you there?*

Yes, you have taken me by surprise, that is all. What you have suggested is new to me. That a soul can live again in another lifetime.

Matthew bit his lip. *We have no time to waste on this. I need you to trust me and do me this favour. This one favour will have a much bigger spiritual pay-off for both of us – that will transcend both our lifetimes.*

Aymer's voice was grave. *I cannot blithely sit back and allow that witch to escape after the crimes she has committed. Do not ask me to do that.*

You must. Maybe he needed to be more persuasive. *Your life is on the line. Mine too and more than that – our immortal soul.*

Only God can decide that – not a witch.

Why did Aymer have to be so difficult? His plan would work if only his past self wasn't so defiant.

His brain worked at double speed. *But if that is the case – then can't you put the fate of the witch in God's hands – let God kill her, if that is what He intends?*

No. It's too risky. How many more ways might she betray us to the Scots before God may intervene? God helps those who help themselves – it is written in the bible.

Aymer could sure be stubborn. He needed to change tack; if not the witch, then maybe he could save Colbyn. *What about the thirty men you took into the oubliette? You're going to kill them all, aren't you? You're going to execute them as a bargaining tool with the Scots.*

Maybe. We haven't yet decided what their fate will be.

He thought of Colbyn; how would he set one soldier apart from the other twenty-nine? They all looked the same: grisly, starved, dirty in their yellow and red colours of Edward Bruce's army.

Time to plead with his past self. *Don't kill them. Use them to negotiate, but then let them go. It will serve you well.*

That would serve the Scots well, not us! We don't surrender to their terms. Never. No surrender!

Why did Aymer have to be so defiant! *Such a phrase is used in my lifetime too, and do you know where it gets us? The politics in our country is polarised. It's the same argument as it was in your time, only it's seven hundred years later. People divided by the differences that they pretend they have from each other. Humans never learn.*

Matthew hesitated, struggling to formulate his thoughts into a convincing argument. *You have to listen, Aymer. Now is the chance to make a difference. You have in your hands a chance to change the course of history, don't you see that? Don't you see how rare and precious that is?*

Aymer was listening; he sensed it. He could picture Aymer, looking downwards at his hands.

My hands, yes. You're right. The power to change the course of the war – and of history – is in my hands.

Did Aymer understand? The connection was gone. All he could do was hope – and trust – that his former self understood the importance of the power he wielded, with his modern knowledge, in the past.

CHAPTER FORTY-TWO

Matthew. Aymer. Parasitic twin Ben. Medieval Colbyn. Failenn. Beollan. Sonya.

Seven.

Seven figures, from past and present.

Seven for death.

Seven hundred and eight. The number of years between torturous medieval past and malevolent present.

1315 AD to 2023 AD.

Seven: death.

Zero: danger.

Eight: birth and liberation.

He understood death. He understood danger. He had seen nothing but death and danger for the past few months of his life; he was sure he had aged a decade from all the stress. Past-life visions, a medieval witch materialising in the present to haunt and torment him, a parasitic twin who had been cut from his body and regenerated into a fully formed corporeal version of his past-life enemy. It was enough to turn a perfectly sane person completely mad.

He had forgotten the silvery, ethereal puddle on the floor. As though on cue, the ectoplasmic pool that stretched five feet across the floor began to rise, as though his attention had impacted it in a psycho-reactive sense. What corpse from the past was left to torment him? None that he could think of: Aymer, Beollan, Failenn and Colbyn had each taken their turn in forming and decaying before him.

Instead of a corpse, the ectoplasmic substance began to form into the silvery outline of a man, as though a 3D printer had produced a model. Colbyn's features were recognisable in the ethereal form, the hollows of its eyes turned towards him. An echoey voice resonated from a trough, like a mouth, in the figure's head.

"Try as you might, you can't change history. You can't change the course of fate. I have won," said ectoplasmic Colbyn.

"You haven't won yet. I'm still here. I'm in contact with Aymer. There is hope for me – and him – and us all yet."

"Aymer won't do as you ask, you have no influence on what has already happened."

He shook his head. "If I can talk to him and get him to understand everything I know, then he can change

all our fates. Isn't that what you want? Don't you want
to live? Doesn't Failenn? Wouldn't it be better if we all
unite and work together to change the past than keep
fighting? I have the power to save us all from a terrible
fate."

"You have no power. Everyone dies. Flesh goes
back to earth. Only the immortal soul lives on. The
battle of our immortal souls has already been won. I
have won."

"You're a ghost – look at you. You're made of
silvery ectoplasm. I'm a real person. My soul is inside
me. The soul is nothing without flesh; the mind is
nothing without the body," he argued.

Ectoplasmic Colbyn threw its head back and
laughed. "I have been leeching your soul out of you
this whole time. You're almost dead. Don't you see
that? The seagull reopened the psychic wound and let
the ghost of us – the foetus-in-foetu – open a portal
with the past.

He was silent, watching his ethereal enemy, his head
filled with neurones stretching out from a ghostly flesh
mass. They invaded his nostrils, corrupted his brain.

"Danger and death. Birth and liberation – of what?"

"You know the answer to that, you don't need me
to tell you."

"You're already reborn – as Ben downstairs. He's a
fresh new life, a blank canvas, wiped clean of the evils
of the past. What more do you want, Colbyn?"

Colbyn's silvery features stretched wide into a
malicious grin. "I have taken the immortal power of
seven souls and condensed into this perfect form that
you see standing before you." The phantasm swept his
hands downwards, gesturing to his body, then spread

them wide. "Now I, along with Failenn in Sonya's body, will finish the campaign we started in 1315."

He barely had time to think what that meant, when the silvery figure of Colbyn turned and walked to the door. Without opening it, the phantasm dissolved through the wood leaving no residue.

What to make of it? Had the life energy from each of the seven figures: Aymer, Ben, Colbyn, Matthew, Sonya, Beollan and Failenn, in each of their lifetimes, been harnessed across time and pooled into the phantasm that had manifested in Colbyn's form? A soldier. A perfect killing machine.

Yes. The psionic connection with the past had backfired. He had allowed Failenn to extract energy from them all, both in the past and in the present. What had he done?

He screamed, expelling every gasp of air that filled his lungs. The scream held so much fear; beyond what his earthly life could harness. His immortal soul cried and twisted in pain. He had given Failenn his power.

There was no energy left in his body. Nothing left to scream with. He was so near the end: of his body, his soul, his life.

His immortal existence.

CHAPTER FORTY-THREE

A cold, numbing pain trickled through Ben's body, as though every nerve had been engulfed by liquid nitrogen. Was it because Matthew was so near the end? They were still connected, whether he liked it or not, as though an astral umbilical cord tethered them together.

"It is done. The transformation is complete." Sonya smiled at him, but it was Failenn's green eyes that glinted with glee. "Your rebirth was incomplete, but now the energy of seven is in you. Seven people, spanning seven centuries."

Instead of elation, panic surfaced. "I can feel Matthew's soul. It isn't dead yet."

A derisive smirk played on her face. "Then he was playing possum upstairs, the devious bastard. Not to worry. His soul will be snuffed out before too long."

Feeling began to return to Ben's body; a warmth as blood pumped life through him. He breathed the lifeforce of seven into his lungs. Adrenaline surged and serotonin at the thought of freedom; freedom from Aymer. From the past.

Sonya closed her eyes and sniffed. "Your smell has changed. There's a sweet scent coming out of you."

His forehead creased. "Sweet? What do you mean?"

"You smelled salty before like sweat. But now you smell sweet. Sweet as the tide of justice."

He grinned at her. It wasn't Sonya who spoke, but Failenn, currently usurping her body; though he had to admit, he rather enjoyed his past-life lover dwelling inside the current tall, slender redheaded form. It added a tantalising spice to their relationship; a new dynamic, like adding a third person to their love-life. *Two is company, three's a crowd.* He cancelled out the proverb in his head with one strike and replaced it with another phrase: *ménage à trois*. Ben, Sonya and Failenn made a welcome trio. Sonya's intellect, Failenn's cunning. It made for an interesting personality.

Matthew would be dead soon and then his transformation would really be complete. Aymer of past and Matthew of present would be vanquished, absorbed by Ben of future.

From the fleshy mass of a foetus-in-foetu, stem cells had taken root.

Stem cells that were capable of human life.

A compound soup of cells with the blueprint of life that had grown and spread, capable of forming every organ in the human body.

Ben's brain had developed, bestowed with the knowledge of seven lives, past and present. A brain that could remember all that had passed in Colbyn's former lifetime and held Failenn's power.

A super brain, equipped with a powerful, muscular body, courtesy of a blood offering to a witch in a past life. Ben's body, reinforced by ectoplasmic manifestation, was stronger than anything alive. It was capable of extracting a debt born of an injustice seven hundred years ago.

***

That momentary panic, that wisp of fear, a last gasp of Matthew that had surfaced within Ben now floated free towards the spare room upstairs. It travelled through the door, a bodiless wave of energy and alighted in the pale, almost lifeless body that lay on the bed.

With a gasp, Matthew's eyes bulged open. He was alive; but barely.

Or was he dead? The ectoplasmic form had taken the last of his remaining energy with it as it had flowed out through the closed door and flowed downstairs, morphing into Ben's living body.

On the other hand, panic swelled in the open cavity of Matthew's nearly deceased body, where seagull-Failenn had pecked, where the ghost of a parasitic twin had emerged from his damaged torso. This was no ordinary panic; it was an existential fear that everything he was in this lifetime, and in any future lifetime, would be wiped out. Disappear, vanish into an astral blackhole from which there would be no escape.

"Aymer, please, I'm begging you. Our fate rests in your hands. My hands are tied. You alone have the power. I have none."

***

"He's still alive. A slice of his consciousness floated out of you. I saw it drift back upstairs. The perfect consciousness is fractured. We have to fix it before it's too late. He might still try to change the course of fate. We can't let him save Aymer and change our destiny." Sonya's eyes were on the ceiling, though her mind seemed to be on the room above.

Ben focused hard, listening too. He didn't hear any sound from the spare room. If a silvery shred of Matthew's soul had drifted back to the pitiful flesh-husk on the bed, then it certainly didn't have the energy to save the wretch's life. Matthew was no threat.

***

Matthew strained with all his might. He thrashed. He gritted his teeth. If Aymer was not going to act now, then he would take over his past-self's body; force his present-day consciousness into Aymer's brain using the tunnel of time. Instead of seeing through Aymer's eyes, as he had witnessed the majority of visions of his past-life until now, he would physically take over control of Aymer's body and change the course of fate. He would save Failenn's life, release Colbyn and the other Scottish hostages back into the care of Edward Bruce's army. He would use his modern knowledge and lead the negotiations to change the course of history, as well as saving the immortal soul that connected them both.

***

"He's alive. The bastard is fighting back. I heard a thump, just now, from that room."

Ben threw the kitchen door wide and bounded into the hallway. But as he started onto the stairs, it was as though a magnet pulled him backwards, tugging from his hips. He strained to lift each foot and set it on the step above, but the effort was momentous.

"What is this sorcery? How is Matthew capable of this? Help me, Failenn."

Why couldn't he move? The cold numbness that had overtaken him before had seized control of his body. It consumed every muscle, bone. Each cell and every atom. The air felt heavy, as though an invisible pull drew everything towards the spare room, the centre of gravity in the house. The cosmic balance would be reset soon. Aymer had caused a void; Matthew would now pay the universal toll. Despite the numbness, he plodded onwards, upwards.

Thunk. One step.

Thunk. At a–

Thunk. Time.

***

The hands of time didn't tick, or even tock. They hammered down with a metallic thunk. Matthew felt himself slipping, falling backwards through the passage of time into another consciousness, when the world was a second younger on the grand scale of life.

It wasn't his life. Not any longer.

Thunk. The metallic clang of yesteryear.

Thunk. The hammer of destiny.

Thunk. The final call of fate.

CHAPTER FORTY-FOUR

Thunk.

Thunk.

Thunk.

As the candle-clock melted, the third and final nail fell to the tabletop with a clatter. The flame flickered and died and in the absence of its meagre light, the passageway was dark and full of an ominous air.

The oubliettes stank. Aymer stopped in front of the heavy, iron gate of the first oubliette that held eight of the thirty Scottish prisoners.

He looked down at the key in his hands. The key to the fate of the men held captive; but more so of one in particular. He could see the one he wanted, huddled near the back, starving and dirty. The prisoner he had his eye on was called Colbyn.

They were all starving: both the Scottish enemy and the soldiers of his garrison alike. All were worn from battle, bone and sinew showing where once there had been strong flesh. Famine and war, war and famine; and now a desperate fate of slow starvation as the Scots outside the castle walls surrounded Carraig Fhearghais, and waited until his garrison were all dead from starvation.

"The power is in my hands. My hands. I alone have the power to change the course of history. I alone have heard a voice that has spoken to me across time and told me of what lies ahead."

His bony, malnourished fingers fumbled with the iron gate. The prisoners inside the oubliette were too weak to look up, never mind try to escape through the open gateway. He left the gate hanging ajar as he shuffled between the chained men, crossed the stony room, and seized Colbyn by his right arm.

"Colbyn, you are to be charged with conspiring with a witch, in a secret pact of treachery against both Edward Bruce's army and the good people of Ulster. How do you plead?"

Colbyn, weak from hunger, looked up at him with bleary eyes, but said nothing.

He continued. "This witch, Failenn, was the daughter of Beollan, Keeper of Grain at Carraig Fhearghais. She has used blood magic – with your own blood – to secure an unnatural victory against my people. How do you plead?

Still no answer. Colbyn let his chin fall forward onto his jutting collarbone.

"Necromancy and pagan runes, imbued with blood onto a clay urn is a crime against God. Your immortal soul is guilty – as is that of the witch Failenn."

A sigh from Colbyn, causing a breeze that stirred the lank hair falling over his face.

"You have paid a heavy price and now owe a blood debt – one that you must pay for with your life." He dragged Colbyn to his feet. "The time has come to collect that debt."

In spite of his emaciated form, he found the energy to haul Colbyn out of the oubliette, up the passageway and out into the courtyard where his fellow soldiers held the witch in the pillory. Despite bending double in the wooden stocks, she had a defiant glint in her eyes, which were fixed on him as he drew near.

"Fate has taken control now. You can't change destiny," she uttered, so that only he could hear.

"Enough from you, witch. I will not be swayed by your occult threats," he spat.

"You heard Matthew's voice, but you didn't listen to his voice," she teased. "Matthew failed."

He would not listen to her ungodly sorcery. "As it is said in the bible, he that is without sin among us, let him cast the first stone at her."

"Sin knows the truth, Sin is always watching," said the witch, directly into his mind, for she hadn't opened her mouth; an unnatural energy flowed in her sharp, green eyes.

Aymer stooped and picked up a rock; a large one that fit in his right fist. He looked closer at it, in his cupped palm. It wasn't a rock. It was a dark reddish-brown urn covered in linear marks. A vessel intended for evil purposes. He lifted his right arm over his shoulder, straight as the arm of a trebuchet, and flung the urn at the witch's face. It pelted her left cheekbone but didn't smash. A blue-black glow emanated from the urn as it rolled aside. Had the evil in it been released? Had her curse on the people of Carraig Fhearghais, and indeed on the serfs across all of Ireland, rebounded? Could there be a chance that the Scottish army might lose their conquest in Ulster?

Blood splattered the left side of her face and an angry red welt appeared where the urn had struck her skin. "You bleed like a woman, but you are no woman, witch," Aymer spat.

Another of his garrison followed suit, casting a stone this time; and another, and another. More welts erupted all over the witch's flesh, the skin raised in angry, red mounds. As her head hung lower, and lower, her energy waning, he noticed that the smile never left her face. The evil in her would never die. It would taunt him until the very end of her life.

A smoky grey wisp escaped from the top of the witch's head. It floated left, rather than upwards, and blended with the blue-black glow that had escaped the urn. The combined energy resonated with a new grey-black colour, pulsating with evil. It rolled and coiled across the courtyard towards him. With a gasp he stepped aside and it missed him, instead engulfing Colbyn. Colbyn gasped and threw his head back before slumping to the ground, the weight of his barely alive body dragging on Aymer's left arm until he was forced to let go of his captive.

The grey-black evil mist lifted from Colbyn's body and drifted onwards across the courtyard. Aymer turned to look behind; transfixed with horror, he saw the other seven prisoners who had also been in the oubliette with Colbyn, had crept out of their prison. He had forgotten to lock the gate after taking Colbyn out. While the garrison had been busy killing the witch, the men had been making their way across the courtyard towards their escape. But not now. The grey-black mist surrounded them, halted them in their tracks; consumed them.

His fault! It was all his fault! Eight prisoners, consumed by evil.

"What is this unearthly smoke?" cried a fellow soldier, his voice ringing with fear.

"It's the soul of the witch trying to corrupt the prisoners," cried another.

"It's worse." He spoke in a slow, solemn tone. "There's a curse on these men, which will be a curse on us all. We have no choice now. We can't use them to negotiate our terms. They must be killed."

"Yes, kill them I say. Aymer speaks the truth," said a third soldier.

"They must be quartered, so that their bodies cannot return to this earth for occult purposes. They must be put to fire. All of them, the witch too. Fire will cleanse them all. Cleanse us all."

CHAPTER FORTY-FIVE

I must save my immortal soul, for myself, and for Matthew in my future. I must save us from an unholy fate. Save my people. Save the land.

Aymer took a deep breath and felt cool, summer air cleanse his lungs.

"Do unto others as you would have them do unto you," he said aloud, calming his heartbeat, stilling his mind.

Another deep breath to clear the smoke from his lungs.

The eight men and one woman no longer looked like humans. They rather resembled chunks of animal flesh that had been cooked.

One more deep breath, to stop the saliva from springing to his lips.

These were people, not animals. Human flesh, not meat.

The garrison were starving. They could not be denied a feast when it was in front of them.

But this was human flesh, not animals.

No, this was no different than cattle. Or pigs.

He shook his head, smacked his own cheek. He was a man of the church, who had been diligent of his studies of the good book in Latin, in what seemed another age on earth. An age before war.

And famine.

Saliva pooled unabated.

What came from the earth would go back to the earth. But these eight men, and one woman had been tainted by evil. If, on the other hand, their flesh was to be eaten and purified, then it would return to the earth in a pure form.

Yes, he was doing it for the good of their immortal souls and his own.

Aymer took a chunk of spit-roasted flesh.

"Goodbye Colbyn," he said, and bit into it.

Above, a flock of seagulls circled lower, waiting for their share of the feast.

EPILOGUE

In an instant, the cold numbness lifted from Ben's legs, and he found himself able to continue his journey upstairs towards the spare bedroom.

"Matthew isn't dead. He's alive and he knows the truth. He has seen the ghastly event through Aymer's eyes," Ben said, more to himself than Sonya, though she trailed closely behind. "I have been set free."

Ben hurried across the landing and pushed the bedroom door open. When the door swung wide, he gasped.

Seagulls. A flock of seagulls had descended on the bed. In between flapping wings, sharp yellow beaks and a flurry of loose, white feathers, Ben couldn't see a thing.

"In the year of our gracious Goddess of the Lunar Light, in the year of 20 and 23, Justice will be served." Sonya's hands flew to her face, making a triangle with her thumbs touching across the bridge of her nose, and forefingers meeting above her brow ridge. Ben watched her peer through the third eye she had made.

"Yes. Justice is being served," said Ben.

"For my father, and for you, and for me," she added.

A rush of wings took to the air as all the birds, but one, flew out the spare bedroom window.

Ben and Sonya turned their attention to the one lone seagull on the bed. It perched on top of scattered bones and hair; all that remained of Matthew.

Sonya turned Failenn's third eye towards the bird. "Yes. Now, as he did to us in a former lifetime, we get to do to him."

Ben understood. It was the bird that had pecked Matthew's wound open, allowing the ghost of the foetus-in-foetu out of him. Ben snatched it with a quick flex of his left hand. Blood spilled over his right hand, staining it bright red. Whether from the bird, or from Matthew inside its belly, he didn't know; but nor did he care. He dragged the flapping bird across the mattress, steadying himself against its powerful wing beats with his body weight on his right hand. The blood left a red handprint on the mattress.

"A red hand – the sign of a victorious warrior. The Red Hand of Ulster. I'm the only chieftain now. I claim this land. My adversary is dead," said Ben, his words drifting into the still bedroom air.

He took the bird downstairs. It fluttered helplessly, beating its wings against his arms, but he held it with a tight grip on its legs.

Ben held the bird's body in his left hand and broke its neck with his right hand. He plucked the bird and chopped up its flesh then threw the chunks into a pot of boiling water and cooked it into a bubbling soup.

"We drink of the urn. What was once met by fire is now cancelled by water. The first of sixteen in our quest for justice," said Sonya.

She handed him the urn in her cupped hands, a smile playing about her mouth, and her eyes glinting green. Sonya's brown eyes were now, and forevermore, green. The witch was in control, not the girl.

Ben ladled broth made of seagull, with a belly full of Matthew, into the urn. He took a sip, closing his eyes to savour justice that had waited for seven hundred and eight years. Justice served warm.

Or cold. An itch, low down in his abdomen niggled at his skin, irritated his body. Ben hitched up his shirt and looked downwards at his well-sculpted abs. He could see red welts across his torso, below the bellybutton, where his appendix would be. With a start, he realised he was looking at a Latin inscription, carved from within his torso.

Tu nihil sine me.

You are nothing without me.

Veniam ad vos.

I am coming for you.

Other books by Leilanie Stewart

The Blue Man: A haunted friendship across the decades

Chill with a Book Premier Readers' Award and Book of the Month winner, February 2023

Two best friends. An urban legend. A sinister curse.

Twenty years ago, horror loving Sabrina told her best friend, Megan, the terrifying Irish folk tale of the Blue Man, who sold his soul to the Devil in vengeance against a personal injustice. What should have been the best summer of their schooldays turned into a waking nightmare, as the Blue Man came to haunt Megan. Sabrina, helpless to save Megan from a path of self-destruction and substance abuse as she sought refuge from the terror, left Belfast for a new life in Liverpool.

Twenty years later, the former friends reunited thinking they had escaped the horrors of the past. Both were pregnant for the first time. Both had lived elsewhere and moved back to their hometown, Belfast. Both were wrong about the sinister reality of the Blue Man, as the trauma of their school days caught up to them – and their families.

Why did the Blue Man terrorise Megan? Was there more to the man behind the urban legend? Was their friendship – and mental health – strong enough to overcome a twenty year curse?

The Fairy Lights: The ghost of Christmas that never was

Author Shout Reader Ready Awards – Recommended Read 2024 winner

When Aisling moves into an old, Edwardian house in the university area of Stranmillis, Belfast, she soon discovers that her student digs are haunted. The house, bought by her grandfather decades ago, is also home to a spirit known by the nickname Jimbo.

As yuletide approaches, and Aisling's Christmas fairy lights attract mischief from Jimbo, she seeks to find out more about the restless entity. With the help of a local psychic and friends from her History with Irish course, Aisling uncovers dark, buried truths. What is the connection with Friar's Bush Graveyard just around the corner? What does Jimbo's dusty book of the Oak King and Holly King, hidden in the attic, have to reveal? What will Aisling's journey into the darkness of the spirit world reveal about Jimbo – and herself?

The Buddha's Bone: A dark psychological journey to find light

Death

Kimberly Thatcher wasn't an English teacher. She wasn't a poet. She wasn't an adventurer. Now she wasn't even a fiancée. But when one of her fellow non-Japanese colleagues tried to make her a victim, she said no.

Cremation

In Japan on a one-year teaching contract at a private English language school, and with her troubled relationship far behind her in London, Kimberly set out to make new friends. She would soon discover the darker side of travelling alone – and people's true intentions.

Rebirth

As she came to question the nature of all those around her – and herself – Kimberly was forced to embark on a soul-searching journey into emptiness. What came next after you looked into the abyss? Could Kimberly overcome the trauma – of sexual assault and pregnancy loss – blocking her path to personal enlightenment along the way, and forge a new identity in a journey of-

Death. Cremation. Rebirth.

Gods of Avalon Road

London, present day.

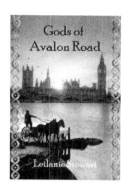

Kerry Teare and her university friend Gavin move to London to work for the enigmatic Oliver Doncaster. Their devious new employer lures them into an arcane occult ritual involving a Golden Horse idol.

Britannia, AD 47.

Aithne is the Barbarian Queen of the Tameses tribes. The Golden Warrior King she loves is known as Belenus. But are the mutterings of the Druids true: is he really the Celtic Sun God himself?

Worlds collide as Oliver's pagan ritual on Mayday summons gods from the Celtic Otherworld of Avalon. Kerry is forced to confront the supernatural deities and corrupt mortals trying to control her life and threatening her very existence.

About the Author:

Leilanie Stewart is an author and poet from Belfast, Northern Ireland. She has written four novels, including award-winning ghost horror, The Blue Man, as well as three poetry collections. Her writing confronts the nature of self; her novels feature main characters on a dark psychological journey who have a crisis of identity and create a new sense of being. She began writing for publication while working as an English teacher in Japan, a career pathway that has influenced themes in her writing. Her former career as an Archaeologist has also inspired her writing and she has incorporated elements of archaeology and mythology into both her fiction and poetry.

In addition to promoting her own work, Leilanie runs Bindweed Magazine, a creative writing literary journal with her writer husband, Joseph Robert. Aside from publishing pursuits, Leilanie enjoys spending time with her husband and their lively literary lad, a voracious reader of sea monster books.

AUTHOR NOTE

Although this story is fictional, some of the locations and events are based on history. I took many trips to Carrickfergus Castle, and was fascinated by the notion that, driven to starvation by the Scottish army under Edward Bruce, the garrison at Carrickfergus may have eaten 8 of the 30 prisoners taken captive. That idea was one of many that I wanted to include in my novel.

Since this is a work of fiction, I'm not required to cite references in the back, as would be necessary in a non-fiction publication; nevertheless, this book required a huge deal of research for the historical chapters, more so than any other novel I have written to date. Therefore, I would like to include acknowledgements to the following books and websites, upon which I relied for background reading:

1. The Wars of the Bruces: Scotland, England and Ireland, 1306-1328 by Colm McNamee
2. Galloglass 1250-1600 by Fergus Cannan
3. A History of Ulster by Jonathan Borden
4. www.craigavonhistoricalsociety.org.uk/rev/kellye nglandulst.php
5. www.historyireland.com/the-bruce-invasions-of-ireland-11
6. www.daera-ni.gov.uk/articles/cattle-imports-gb
7. www.catherinehanley.co.uk/historical-background/arming-a-knight-in-the-thirteenth-century
8. www.heraldry.sca.org/names/namesfrom13thcen turyScotlandParliamentaryRecords.html
9. www.behindthename.com/submit/names/usage/medieval-irish

ACKNOWLEDGEMENTS

I am fortunate to have a great team to help prepare my books for release into the world. Immense thanks to my fabulous hubby, fellow writer, editor and biggest bibliophile I know, Joseph Robert, for lending a critical eye to this book and helping catch historical details that needed fleshed out from their bare bones (cheesy pun intended). Thanks to Heather for the brilliant proofreading, as always, and to Kendra Sneddon and Jeanne Bertille for the ARC read support.

I'm grateful to have dedicated readers, who also help to share and promote my social media posts. Marketing for an Indie author is always an ongoing word of mouth battle, so thanks to all of the following for the support: Zeena; Alison Dowdell and David Smith.

Among the writing community, I have made some amazing fellow author friends, who I have learned much from and shared support with. A shout-out to all of the following fab authors: Amanda Sheridan, Ricardo Sanchez, Megan A. Dell, Isobel Reed, Chloe Gilholy and Rosalind Barden for reading my books and helping to promote my social media posts. Thank you and hope we can actually meet in person someday.

Thanks also to little KJ for being a super-duper literary assistant when I needed to focus and get my book done. Hope I made it up to you with all the day trips afterwards!

AND OF COURSE...

Last, but not least, thanks to you, dear reader, for buying my book. Hearing your thoughts on my writing keeps me motivated to write more books, so just to let you know that I appreciate you taking the time to read and review my books. It means more than you know.

Printed in Great Britain
by Amazon

44714010R00158